# FALLING FOR
# HER ARMY DOC

## DIANNE DRAKE

**MILLS & BOON**

First published in Great Britain 2020
by Mills & Boon, an imprint of HarperCollins*Publishers*
1 London Bridge Street, London, SE1 9GF

Large Print edition 2020

© 2020 Dianne Despain

ISBN: 978-0-263-08578-5

**MIX**
Paper from
responsible sources
**FSC** **FSC C007454**
www.fsc.org

This book is produced from independently certified FSC™ paper to ensure responsible forest management. For more information visit www.harpercollins.co.uk/green.

Printed and bound in Great Britain
by CPI Group (UK) Ltd, Croydon, CR0 4YY

I dedicate this book to Mr. Kahawaii, who took me into his amazing world for a little while.

# CHAPTER ONE

SHE LOOKED BEAUTIFUL, standing outside in the garden, catching the morning light. He watched her every day about this time. She'd take her walk, sit for a few minutes on the stone retaining wall surrounding the sculpted flowers, then return to the building.

Once, he'd wondered what weighed her down so heavily. She had that look—the one he remembered from many of his patients, and probably even more he didn't remember. She—Lizzie, she'd told him her name was—always smiled and greeted him politely. But there was something behind that smile.

Of course, who was he to analyze? It had taken a photo he'd found among his things to remind him that he'd been engaged. Funny how his memory of her prior to his accident was blurred. Nancy was a barely recognizable face in a world he didn't remember much of. And, truthfully, he couldn't even recall how or why he'd become engaged to her. She didn't seem his type—too flighty, too intrusive. Too greedy.

Yet Lizzie, out there in the garden, seemed perfect. Beautiful. Smart. In tune with everything around her.

So what wasn't he getting here? Had he changed so much that the type of woman who'd used to attract him didn't now? And taking her place was someone…more like Lizzie?

Dr. Mateo Sanchez watched from the hospital window until Lizzie left the garden, then he drew the blinds and went back to bed. He didn't have a lot of options here, as a patient. Rest, watch the TV, rest some more. Go to therapy. Which somehow he never quite seemed to do.

This was his fourth facility since he'd been shipped from the battlefield to Germany, and nothing was working. Not the therapy. Not his attitude. Not his life. What he wanted to know they wouldn't tell him. And what he didn't want to know just seemed to flood back in when he didn't want it to.

The docs were telling him to be patient, that some memory would return while some would not. But he wanted a timeline, a calendar on his wall where he could tick off the days until he was normal again.

He reached up and felt the tiny scar on his head. Whatever normal was. Right now, he didn't know. There was nothing for him to hold on to. No one there to ground him. Even Nancy hadn't stayed around long after she'd discovered he didn't really know her.

In fact, his first thought had been that she was a nurse, tending him at his bedside. She'd been good when he'd asked for a drink of water, even when he'd asked for another pillow, and she'd taken his criticism when she'd told him she couldn't give him a pain pill.

This had gone on for a week before she'd finally confessed that she wasn't his nurse, but his fiancée. And then, in another week, she'd been gone. She wasn't the type to do nursing care in the long term, she'd said. And unfortunately, all she could see ahead of her was nursing care, a surgeon who could no longer operate, when what she'd wanted was a surgeon who could provide a big home, fancy cars, and everything else he'd promised he'd give her.

So, he knew the what and the when of his

accident. What he *didn't* know was the annoying part. As a surgeon he needed to know all aspects of his patients' conditions, even the things that didn't seem to matter. It was called being thorough. But for him…

*"Giving you the answers to your life could imprint false memories,"* his neurologist Randy always said, when he asked. And he was right, of course. That was something he did remember. Along with so many of his basic medical skills—the ones he'd learned early on in his career.

The more specific skills, though… Some of them were still there. Probably most of them. But in pulling them out of his memory he hesitated sometimes. Thought he remembered but wasn't sure of himself.

*Wait a minute. Let me consult a textbook before I remove your gall bladder.*

Yeah, right. Like *that* was going to work in surgery.

He looked up and saw Lizzie standing in his doorway, simply observing him. Probably trying to figure out what to do with him.

"Hello," he said, not sure what to make of this.

She was the house primary care physician—not his doctor, not even a neurologist. Meaning she had no real reason to be here unless he needed a vaccination or something.

"I've seen you watch me out in the garden. I was wondering if you'd like to come out with me for a while later…breathe some fresh air, take a walk?"

"Who's prescribing that?" he asked suspiciously.

"You are—if that's what you want to do. You're not a prisoner here, you know. And your doctor said it might be a good idea… that it could help your…" She paused.

"Go ahead and say it. My disposition."

"I understand from morning staff meetings that you're quite a handful."

"Nothing else to do around here," he said. "So, I might as well improve upon my obnoxious level. It's getting better. In fact, I think I'll soon be counted amongst the masters."

"To what outcome?"

He shrugged. "See, that's the thing. For me, there *are* no outcomes."

"If that's how you want it. But I'm not your

doctor and you're not my problem. So, take that walk with me or not."

"And tomorrow? What happens to me tomorrow?"

"Honestly? I'm a one-day-at-a-time girl. Nothing's ever guaranteed, Mateo. If I get through the day, tomorrow will take care of itself."

"Well, I like seeing ahead. And now, even behind."

"To each his own," she said nonchalantly.

"Which implies what?" he asked, feeling a smile slowly crossing his face. Lizzie was... *fun*. Straight to the point. And challenging.

"You know exactly what it implies, Mateo. In your effort to see 'behind,' as you're calling it, you're driving the staff crazy. They're afraid of you. Not sure what to do with you. And that false smile of yours is beginning to wear thin."

"Does it annoy you?" he asked.

"It's beginning to."

"Then my work here is done," he said, folding his arms across his chest.

He wanted clothes—real clothes. Not these blue and green things that were passed off as hospital gowns. Those were for sick people. He wasn't sick. Just damaged. A blood clot on his brain, which had been removed, and a lingering pest called retrograde amnesia. That kind of damage deserved surfer shorts and a Hawaiian shirt, seeing as how he was in Hawaii now.

"And my work has nothing to do with you. I was just trying to be friendly, but you're too much of a challenge to deal with. And, unfortunately, what should have been a simple yes or no is now preventing me from seeing my patients."

She sure was pretty.

It was something he'd thought over and over about Lizzie. Long, tarnished copper hair. Curly. Soft too, he imagined. Brown eyes that could be as mischievous as a kitten or shoot daggers, depending on the circumstance. And her smile… It didn't happen too often, he'd noticed. And when it did, it didn't light up the proverbial room. But it sure did light up his day.

"And how would I be doing that? I'm here, wearing these lovely clothes, eating your gourmet green slime food, putting up with your hospital's inane therapy."

"And by 'putting up with,' you mean not showing up for?" She took a few more steps into the room, then went to open the blinds.

"In the scheme of my future life, what will it do for me?"

"Maybe nothing. Maybe everything."

"No vagaries here, Lizzie. Be as specific as I have to be every time I answer someone's orientation questions. 'Do you remember your name?' 'Where are you?' 'What's the date?' 'Who's the current President?'"

"Standard protocol, Mateo. You know that." She turned back to face him. "But you make everything more difficult than it has to be."

She brightened his day in a way he'd never expected. "So why me? You're not my doctor, but you've obviously chosen me for some special attention."

"My dad was a military surgeon, like you were. Let's just say I'm giving back a little."

"Did he see combat?"

"Too many times."

"And it changed him," Mateo said, suddenly serious.

"It might have—but if it did it was something he never let me see. And he never talked about it."

"It's a horrible thing to talk about. The injuries. The ones you can fix…the ones you can't. In my unit they were rushed in and out so quickly I never really saw anything but whatever it was I had to fix. Maybe that was a blessing."

He shut his eyes to the endless parade of casualties who were now marching by him. This was a memory he didn't want, but he was stuck with it. And it was so vivid.

"Were you an only child?" he asked.

Lizzie nodded. "My mom couldn't stand the military life. She said it was too lonely. So, by the time I was five she was gone, and then it was just my dad and me."

"Couldn't have been easy being a single parent under his circumstances. I know *I* wouldn't have wanted to drag a kid around with me when I was active. Wouldn't have been fair to the kid."

"He never complained. At least, not to me. And what I had…it seemed normal."

"I complain to everybody."

In Germany, after his first surgery, it hadn't

occurred to him that his memory loss might be permanent. He'd been too busy dealing with the actual surgery itself to get any more involved than that. That had happened after he'd been transferred to Boston for brain rehab. Then he'd got involved. Only it hadn't really sunk in the way it should have. But once they'd got him to a facility in California, where the patients had every sort of war-related brain injury, that was when it had occurred to him that he was just another one of the bunch.

How could that be? That was the question he kept asking himself over and over. He had become one of the poor unfortunates he usually treated. A surgeon without his memory. A man without his past.

"You're a survivor who uses what he has at his disposal to regain the bits and pieces of himself he's lost. Or at least that's what you could be if you weren't such a quitter."

"A quitter?"

Maybe he was, since going on was so difficult. But did Lizzie understand what it was like to reach for a memory you assumed would be there and come up with nothing? And he was one of the lucky ones. Physically, he was fine, and his surgery had gone well. He'd healed well, too. But he couldn't get past that one thing that held him back…who was he, *really*?

Suddenly Mateo was tired. It wasn't even noon yet and he needed a nap. Or an escape.

"That walk this evening…maybe. If you can get me some real clothes."

Lizzie chuckled. "I *should* say you'll have to wear your hospital pajamas, but I'll see what I can do."

"No promises, Lizzie. I don't make promises I can't keep, and who knows what side of the pendulum my mood will be swinging on later."

"Whatever suits you," she said, then left the room.

Even though he hated to see her go, what he needed was to be left alone—something he'd told them over and over. He needed time to figure out just how big a failure he was, medically speaking. And what kind of disappointment he was to his mother, who'd worked long and hard to get him through medical school. The arthritis now crippling her hands showed that.

There was probably a long list of other people he'd let down, too, but thankfully he couldn't remember it. Except his own name—

right there at the top. He was Dr. Mateo Sanchez—a doctor with retrograde amnesia. And right now that was all he cared to know. Everything else—it didn't matter.

She was not getting involved. It didn't usually work. Didn't make you happy, either. Didn't do a thing. At least in her case it never had.

Lizzie's mom had walked out when she was barely five, so no involvement there. And her dad… Well, he'd loved her. But her father had been a military surgeon, and that had taken up most of his time. While he'd always said he wanted to spend more time with her, it hadn't happened. So no involvement with him, either, for a good part of her life.

Then there had been her husband. Another doctor, but one who wouldn't accept that she didn't want to be a surgeon like him. He was a neurosurgeon and, to him, being a primary care physician meant being…*lesser.* He did surgeries while she did cuts and bruises, he'd always say. Brad had never failed to show his disappointment in her, so she'd failed there, too. Meaning, what was the point?

None, that Lizzie could think of. But that

was OK. She got along, designed her life the way she wanted it to be, and lived happily in the middle of it. Living in the middle was good, she decided. It didn't take you far, but it didn't let you down, either.

She wondered about Mateo, though. She knew he watched her in the garden every morning. Knew he'd asked questions about her. But the look on his face…there was no confidence there. Something more like fear. Which was why she'd asked him out for a walk this evening. He needed more than the four walls of his hospital room, the same way her father had needed more.

But her father had been on a downward spiral with Alzheimer's. Mateo was young, healthy, had a lot of years of life ahead of him— except he was getting into the habit of throwing away the days. It was hard seeing that, after watching the way her father had deteriorated.

But to get involved…? They weren't friends. Weren't even doctor-patient. Weren't anything. But she'd been watching the watcher for weeks now, and since she'd be going on holiday shortly what would it hurt to get involved for once? Or, in this case, to take a simple evening walk?

Watching Mateo walk toward her now, she thought he struck her as a man who would have taken charge. His gait was strong, purposeful. And he was a large man—massive muscles on a well-defined body. He'd taken care of himself. You didn't get that physique by chance. Yet now he was stalled, and that didn't fit. To look at him was to think he had his life together—it was in the way he carried himself. But there was nothing together about him, not one little piece. And he was sabotaging himself by not trying.

Many of the staff's morning meetings lately had opened with: *"What should we do about Mateo?"*

The majority wanted him out of there. Even his own doctor didn't care. But Lizzie was his advocate because he deserved this chance. Like her dad had, all those times someone had tried to convince her to put him away. That was exactly what they wanted to do with Mateo, and while neurology wasn't her specialty, she did know that some types of brain trauma took a long time to sort themselves out.

But beds here were at a premium. The waiting list was long, and military veterans always went to the top of the list. There was no guarantee they'd stay there, though, especially if they acted the way Mateo did.

He was never mean. Never outright rude, even though he was always on the edge of it. In fact, he smiled more than anybody she'd ever seen. But he refused to try, and that was ultimately going to get in the way, since there were other veterans who could have his bed and display more cooperation.

The waiting line for each and every bed was eight deep, Janis always reminded her, when she was so often the only one at the meeting table who defended him. His bed could be filled with the snap of her fingers, and that was what she had to impress upon Mateo or he'd be out.

Truthfully, Lizzie was worried about Mateo's progress. Or rather his lack of it. His time was indeed running out, and there was serious talk of transferring him elsewhere. He knew that, and it didn't faze him. Not one little bit. Or if it did, he hid it well. Making her wonder why she tried so hard to advocate for a man who didn't advocate for himself.

"Well, you look good in real clothes," she said as he walked up to the reception hub where she'd been waiting.

He spun around the way a model on a runway would, then took a bow as a couple of passing nurses applauded him. "It's good to feel human again."

"You're allowed out in the garden any time, Mateo. All you have to do is ask and someone will walk along with you."

"But today I scored you." He leaned in toward her and whispered, "Who happens to be the prettiest doctor in this hospital."

"Save the flattery for someone else, Mateo. All I'm doing is trying to chart a doctor's note saying you were cooperative for once. So far there aren't any of those on record."

Staff were tired of sugar-coating what they said about him and had started opting for snarky comments instead. In their defense, they were a highly dedicated lot who were bound to their jobs by the need to make improvements in patients' lives—physically and emotionally. And, while Mateo might make them smile, he also frustrated them by pushing them to the limit.

Lizzie nudged a wheelchair in his direction.

"You know I can walk," he said.

"Of course, you can, but…hospital policy. If I take a patient outside, they must go by wheelchair or else I'll be in trouble. In other words, comply, or give back the clothes and go to bed."

"Comply? Easier said than done," he said, not budging from where he was standing at the nurses' hub. "Especially when you're treating me like an invalid."

In truth, he'd prefer not to step outside—or in his case, be wheeled. There were too many things reminding him of how much he'd forgotten. Most days he wasn't in the mood to deal with it. Staying in bed, watching TV, playing video games, sleeping…that was about the extent of his life now.

Except Lizzie. She was the bright spot. And she was asking him out…no way he could turn that down.

"Isn't that how you're treating yourself?" she asked. "We've designed a beautiful program for you here—took days going over it and tweaking it. It's a nice balance for what you've got going on, yet have you ever, just once, referred to it? Daily walks in the garden, for instance? It's on there, Mateo. And work-outs in the gym. But I'll bet you tossed the program in the trash as soon as you received it.

"Might have. Don't remember."

"Saying you've forgotten has become an easy excuse because retrograde amnesia is about forgetting things in the past. Not in the future, or even now. What you're not retaining right now is left over from your brain surgery, but that will improve in time. With some effort. If you let it. Also, if you don't care about your past you can walk out of here right now—a new man with a clean slate. You're healthy, and with some caution you're basically healed. Your destiny at this point is up to you. You can go, if that's what you want. But I don't think it is, because I believe you still want help with your memory loss, as well as trying to recall as much as you can about your life."

"Oh, you mean I want to remember things like how to repair a hernia?"

"It's all in there," she said, tapping her own

head. "Like you've been told. Unless you missed your session that day, procedural things aren't normally lost. Life things are. And, as you already know, you do still have a little bit of head-banging going on after the surgery. But that's not even significant at this point. Your attitude is, though."

"Head-banging would be your professional diagnosis?"

Why the hell did he do this? He didn't like it, but sometimes the belligerence just slipped out anyway. And Lizzie was only trying to help. He'd heard it whispered that she was the only one standing between him and being sent elsewhere.

"It would be the way *you* described your headaches when you were first admitted. But you remember that, Mateo. Which means you're in one of your moods now. You think you can smile your way through it and maybe the staff won't notice that you're not working toward a better recovery? Well, I notice. Every little detail." She smiled back at him. "I'd be remiss in my duties if I didn't."

"So, I'm part of your duty?"

"You're one of the patients here. That's all.

Whatever I choose to do, like go for a walk with you, is because I understand where you are right now."

"*Do* you, Lizzie?" he asked, his voice turning dark. "Do you really? I mean, even if I do retain knowledge of the procedural side of the surgeries I used to perform, would you honestly want a surgeon who comes to do your appendectomy and doesn't even remember what kind of suture he prefers?"

Lizzie laughed, giving the wheelchair one more push toward him. This time it bumped his knees, so he could no longer ignore it.

"Sometimes I wonder if someone should change your diagnosis to retrograde amnesia with a secondary symptom of being overly dramatic. You're a challenge, Mateo, that's for sure. And, just between us, an open appendectomy skin closure works best with an absorbable intradermic stitch. Although if you're doing the procedure laparoscopically, all it takes is a couple of dissolvable stitches on the inside and skin glue on the outside."

"And you know this because…?"

"I've done a few stitches in my time. That's part of being a PCP. So quit being so dramatic.

It doesn't score points with me, if that's what you're trying to do."

Well, he might have gaps in his memory, including the kind of women he'd been drawn to, but Lizzie certainly held his attention now. Petite, bouncy. Smart. Serious as hell. And that was the part that didn't escape him. Lizzie Peterson was a great big bundle of formidable perfection all tied up in a small package.

Maybe that was what intrigued him the most. He couldn't picture himself with someone like her. Of course, in his recent spotty memory he couldn't picture himself with anybody, including his former fiancée.

"Not overly dramatic. I'm allergic to flowers, which is why I don't want to go to the garden."

"Says who?"

"Says me."

"Then why, just a few minutes ago, did you want to go out?"

"Maybe I wasn't allergic a few minutes ago. Maybe it was a sudden onset aversion."

"Well, it's your choice, Mateo. Your life is out there somewhere. Maybe it's not the one you want, but it's the one you're going to be stuck with. You can make your own choices with it, but what you do now will affect what you do later on. And there is a 'later on' coming up. You can't keep postponing it indefinitely."

She started to walk away but turned back for a final word. She smiled when she saw that he was in the wheelchair, ready to go. Why not? he thought. Nothing else was happening in his life. So why not take a stroll in the garden? Or, in his case, a roll.

He gave Lizzie a deliberate scowl, which turned so quickly into a smile it almost caught her off-guard. "Is there any way I can talk you out of the wheelchair?"

"Nope. I play by the hospital rules and you play by my rules. So, here's the deal. You cooperate."

"Or what?"

"That's all there is to it. You cooperate."

"Isn't a deal supposed to be two-sided?"

"Maybe your deals are, but mine aren't. I like getting my way, Mateo. And when I don't, I'm the one who gets grumpy. Trust me—my grumpy out-grumpys yours any day of the week, so don't try me."

He liked Lizzie. Trusted her. Wanted to impress her even though that was a long way from happening. "OK. Well…if that's all you're offering."

"A walk is a walk, Mateo. Nothing else. So don't go getting ideas."

"You mean this is a pity walk?"

"Something like that. You cooperate and I'll do my best to help you. If you don't cooperate…" She smiled. "I'm sure you can guess the rest."

He could, and he didn't like it. This was a good facility, and as a doctor he recognized that. But as a patient he didn't even recognize himself—and that was the problem. When he looked in the mirror, he didn't know the face that looked back. The eyes, nose and mouth were the same, but there was nothing in his eyes. No sign of who he was or used to be.

And he was just plain scared.

"Big date? You wish," she said on her way out through the door, pushing Mateo in front of her.

Today was Lizzie's thirteenth day on without a break. But she had her nights to herself and found that if she worked hard enough during the day she could sleep through her night-time demons. So, she worked until she was ready to drop, often stopped by The Shack for something tall and tropical, then went home and slept. So far it was working. Thoughts of her dad's death weren't invading every empty moment as much as they'd used to.

Leaning back to the wall, just outside the door, Mateo extricated himself from his wheelchair—which was totally against the rules.

"Is he getting to you?" Janis Lawton asked, stopping to hand Lizzie a bottle of water.

Janis was chief of surgery at Makalapua Pointe Hospital. The one in charge. The one who made the rules and made sure they weren't broken. And the one who was about to send Mateo to another facility on the mainland if he wasn't careful.

"I know the nurses are having problems with him." Janis leaned against the wall next to Lizzie and fixed her attention on Mateo, who'd rolled his chair off the walkway and seemed to be heading for the reflecting pond. "But the thing is, he's so darned engaging and nice most of the time. Then when he's not co-operative, or when he's refusing therapy... It's hard justifying why he's here when my waiting list is so long."

"Because he needs help. Think about what you'd do if you suddenly couldn't be a surgeon anymore."

"I do, Lizzie. All the time. And that's why Mateo keeps getting the benefit of the doubt. I understand exactly what's happening. The rug is being pulled out from under him." She held up her right hand, showing Lizzie a massive scar. "That was almost me. It took me a year of rehab to get back to operating and in the early days... Let's just say that I was more like Mateo than anyone could probably imagine. But as director of the hospital I have some lines I must draw. And Mateo isn't taking that seriously. Maybe you could...?"

Lizzie held up her hand to stop the older woman. "It's an evening walk. That's all. No agenda. No hospital talk, if I can avoid it."

Like the walks she used to take with her dad, even in the days when he hadn't remembered who she was. It had been cathartic anyway. Had let her breathe all the way down to her soul.

"The way Mateo is happens when you don't

know who you are." The way her dad had gotten. The less he'd remembered, the more uncooperative he'd become—and, while Alzheimer's was nothing like amnesia, she was reminded of the look she'd seen so often on her dad's face when she looked at Mateo. The look that said *lost*. And for Mateo, such an esteemed surgeon, to have this happen to him...

"You're not getting him mixed up with your dad, are you?" Janis asked.

Lizzie laughed outright at the suggestion. "No transference going on here! My dad was who he was, Mateo is who he is. And I do know the difference. My dad was lost in his mind. Mateo is lost in his world." She looked out at Mateo, who was now sitting on the stone wall, waiting for her.

"You do realize he's supposed to be in a wheelchair, don't you?" said Janis.

"But do *you* realize how much he doesn't like being treated like an invalid? Why force him across that line with something so trivial as a wheelchair?"

"Well, just so you know, your *friend* isn't on steady footing and he might be best served in another facility."

"This is his fourth facility, Janis. He's running out of options."

"So am I," she said, pushing herself off the wall, her eyes still fixed on Mateo, whose eyes were fixed right back on Janis. "And with you about to take leave for a while…"

That *was* a problem. She'd signed herself off duty for a couple of weeks. There were things in her own life she needed to figure out.

Was this where she wanted to stay, with so many sad memories still fighting their way through? And hospital work—it wasn't what she'd planned to do. She liked the idea of a small local clinic somewhere. Treating patients who might not have the best medical services available to them. Could she actually have something like that? Or was she already where she was meant to be?

Sure, it was an identity crisis mixed in with a professional crisis, but working herself as hard as she did there was no time left to weigh both sides—stay or go? In these two weeks of vacation there would be plenty of time for that—time to clear her mind, time to relax, time to be objective about her own life. It was a lot to sort out, but she was looking forward to it.

Everybody had choices to make, and so far, all her choices had been about other people. What did her husband want? What did her dad need? But the question was: What did Elizabeth Peterson want and need? And what would have happened if she'd chosen differently a year ago?

Well, for starters, her dad might still be alive. That was the obstacle she could never get past. But maybe now, after the tide had washed it all out to sea, that was something she could work on, too. Guilt—the big flashing light that always shone on the fact that her life wasn't in balance. And she had no idea how to restore that balance.

"I thought we were going to walk?" Mateo said, approaching her after Janis had gone inside.

"Did you *have* to break the rule about the wheelchair in front of Janis?" Lizzie asked, taking the hand Mateo offered her when she started to stand up.

"Does it matter? I'm already branded, so does it matter what I do when decisions are being made without my input?"

The soft skin of his hand against hers… It

was enough to cause a slight shiver up her spine—and, worse, the realization that maybe she was ready for that aspect of her life to resume. The attraction. The shivers. Everything that came after.

She'd never had that with Brad. Their marriage had turned cold within the first month. Making love in the five spare minutes he had every other Thursday night and no PDA—even though she would have loved holding hands with him in public. Separate bedrooms half the time, because he'd said her sleeping distracted him from working in bed.

But here was Mateo, drop-dead gorgeous, kind, and friendly, even though he tried to hide it. All in all, he was very distracting. How would he be in a relationship? Not like Brad, she supposed. Brad was always in his own space, doing everything on his own terms, and she had become his afterthought. There was certainly no happily-ever-after in being overlooked by the man who was supposed to love you.

Not that it had made much of a difference, as by the time she'd discovered her place in their marriage she'd already been part-way out the door, vowing never to make that mistake again.

But was that what she really wanted? To spend her life alone? Devote herself to her work? Why was it that one mistake should dictate the rest of her life?

This was another thing to think about during her time off. The unexpected question. Could she do it again if the right man came along? And how could she tell who was right?

Perhaps by trusting her heart? With Brad, it had been more of a practical matter. But now maybe it was time to rethink what she really wanted and how to open herself up to it if it happened along.

Shutting her eyes and rubbing her forehead against the dull headache setting in, it wasn't blackness Lizzie saw. It was Mateo. Which made her head throb a little harder. But also caused her heart to beat a little faster.

# CHAPTER TWO

"I'D CLAIM AMNESIA, but I really don't know the names of most flowers. The purple and white ones...

"Orchids," Lizzie filled in.

"I know what orchids are." Mateo reached over the stone wall and picked one, then handed it to Lizzie. "There's probably a rule against picking the flowers, but you need an... *orchid* in your hair."

She took it and tucked it behind her right ear. "Right ear means you're available. Left means you're taken."

"How could someone like you not be taken?" he asked, sitting down next to her on the stone wall surrounding the garden.

Behind them were beautiful flowers in every color imaginable, with a long reflecting pond in the background. One that stretched toward the ocean.

"Because I don't want to be taken. It's one

of those been-there-done-that situations, and I can still feel the sting from it, so I don't want to make the wound any worse.

"That bad?"

"Let's just say that on a rating of one through ten, I'd need a few more numbers to describe it. So, you haven't been…?"

"I was engaged briefly—apparently. Don't really have any memory of it other than a few flashes, and those aren't very flattering. Definitely not my type, from the little I recall."

"Maybe with your head injury your type changed. That can happen with brain damage. People are known to come out the other side very different from what they were when they went in. Could be the Fates giving you a second chance."

"You can't just have a normal conversation, can you? You turn everything into work."

"Because that's what I *do*."

"That's *all* you do, Lizzie. You come in early, leave late, and probably sandwich some sleep in there somewhere. I lived that schedule in Afghanistan too often, and it catches up to you."

"But this isn't about me, Mateo."

"First-year Med School. 'Treating a patient is as much about you as it is the patient.' Even though some of my patients came in and out so fast they never even saw me, I worked hard to make every one of them feel that they were in good hands, even if those hands were exhausted. But you… There's a deep-down tiredness behind the facade you put on, and it shows in your eyes. And I don't think it's physical so much as something else."

"It's just an accumulation of things. Tough decisions. My dad's death. Things I've wanted I haven't had. Things I've had I haven't wanted." She gave him a weak smile. "You're very perceptive for a man who claims amnesia at the drop of a hat."

"Straightforward talk, honesty…that's what I was all about, Lizzie. Have to be when you're out on the battlefield making quick decisions and performing life-changing procedures." He sighed. "In the end, when you're all they've got, the only real thing that counts is your word."

"Was it difficult…practicing like that?"

"Isn't it what your dad did?"

She shook her head. "He had rank, which got

him assigned to a base hospital. He was the one who took the casualties that people like you had fixed after you sent them on."

"Wouldn't it be crazy if our paths had crossed somewhere? Yours and mine?"

"He kept me pretty isolated from that part of his life. If our paths had crossed it would have been somewhere like that little *bäckerei* on Robsonstrasse in Rhineland-Palatinate. We lived in a little flat about a block from there, and I loved getting up early and going for a Danish, or even a raspberry-filled braid."

"The plum cake there was always my favorite. A little bit sweet, a little bit tart."

"So, you've been there?" Lizzie asked, smiling over the shared memory.

"When I had time. My trips in and out were pretty quick, but I started getting a taste for the plum cake about the same time I stepped on the plane to go there, so that was always my first stop."

"Small world," Lizzie said. "Almost like a fairy tale...where the Princess meets the Prince in the most improbable way, then they have battles to fight to get to each other. You know—the love-conquers-all thing, starting with a fruit Danish and plum cake."

"And the rest of the story in your little world?" he asked. "Do they ever get to their happily-ever-after, or do they eat their cakes alone forever?"

"Let's see..." she said. "So, their paths crossed at the bakery... His eyes met hers— love at first sight, of course. It always happens that way in a nice romantic story. But since the hero of my story was a soldier prince, their time was fleeting. Passionate, but brief. And the kisses...?"

"Were they good?"

"The best she'd ever known. But she was young, and very inexperienced. Oh, and she'd never kissed a real man before. He was her first. Her other kisses had come from boys in the village...no comparison to the kisses of a man."

It was nice, putting herself in the place of a young village maiden. Yes, Mateo's kisses would definitely be those of a real man. She could almost imagine how they would taste on her own lips.

"Was he her first true love?"

Lizzie nodded. "Of course he was. But, the way as many war stories end, they were separated. He was sent somewhere else and her heart was broken."

"Badly, or would she eventually heal?"

"I don't think you ever heal when you've lost the love of your life. But she went after him. She was strong that way."

"*Then* true love prevailed?"

"In my story, yes."

"And they lived happily ever after?"

"As happily-ever-after as any two lovers could with six children. A house in the country. Maybe a few dairy cows."

"Or just a couple of children, a house on a beach in Hawaii, no cows allowed?"

"Nice dream," she said on a sigh. "And I'd kill for a blueberry Danish right now."

Mateo started to slide his hand across the ledge on which they were seated—not so much to hold her hand, but just to brush against it. But either she saw it coming and didn't want it, or she was still caught up in her fairy tale, because just as he made his approach she stood, then turned toward the beach.

"We used to come here when I was a child.

It's grown up a lot. Not much tourism back then."

"Is there any one place you call home, Lizzie?"

She shook her head. "Not really. Home was where we were or where we were going. And you?"

"A small village near Guadalajara, originally. Then wherever my mother could get work after we came to the States."

"Is she…?"

"She's got some health problems…can't travel anymore. But we chat almost every day, and someone at the facility is helping her learn how to video chat."

"Does she know about your injury?"

Mateo shook his head. "Her life was hard enough because of me. Why add to it if I don't have to?"

"After what my dad went through with his Alzheimer's, I think you're doing the right thing."

"Now, about that walk…"

He would have been good doctor. She was sure of that. And she was touched by his caring attitude toward his mother. Even toward *her*.

This wasn't the Mateo who refused his treatments or walled himself into his room like a recluse. This was someone entirely different. Someone she hadn't expected but was glad she'd found.

"Well, if we go one way we'll run into a shaved ice concession, and if we go the other way it's The Shack."

"And The Shack is…?"

"Fun, loud, dancing, music, watered-down drinks for the tourists… Pretty much a place I shouldn't be taking you."

"Which is exactly why I'm taking *you*."

"Two-drink limit, Mateo. Beer, preferably. You're not on any prohibitive meds, but…"

"I was wondering when the doctor would return."

"The doctor never left."

"Oh, yes, she did," he said, smiling. "And I was the one who got to see it happen."

It was well into the evening—"her time," as she called it. She really needed to go home and rest. But now that he was out here, she wanted to keep him here. Because while he was here he wasn't inside the hospital, getting into trouble. Even his good looks—which everybody noticed—weren't enough to change their minds, and right now the mindset was not in Mateo's favor. Presently she was too exhausted to deal with it, so this little time out was badly needed. Probably for both of them.

Lizzie took a quick appraisal, even though she knew what he looked like. But she liked his dark look. The muscles. The smooth chest. And his hands...large, but gentle—the hands of a surgeon. How would they be as the hands of a lover? she wondered, as he spotted her amongst the crowd, then came her direction.

"I saw you staring at me," he said, as a couple of young women from the bar watched him with obvious open invitation.

Who could blame them? Lizzie thought. He was the best-looking man there.

"Not staring. Just watching to make sure you weren't doing something that would embarrass you and cost me my job."

"But you're off duty."

"And you're still a patient of the hospital."

"But not your patient, Lizzie. And therein lies the distinction." He grabbed a cold beer from a passing server and handed it to Lizzie. "Do you ever allow yourself to have fun?"

"Do you ever allow yourself to *not* have fun?" she asked, wondering if, in his previous life, he'd been a party boy.

He held up his bottle to clink with hers, but she stepped back before that could happen.

"You're a beautiful woman, Lizzie. Prettier than anyone else here. And you're smart. But if I were your doctor I'd prescribe more fun in your life—because even when you're standing in the middle of it, you can't see it."

"Then it's a good thing you're not my doctor, isn't it?"

Mateo reached over and took Lizzie's beer, then took a swig of it.

"That's your limit," she warned him.

"Actually, it's one over—but who's counting?"

Lizzie shook her head, caught between smiling and frowning. "I shouldn't have to count. Somewhere in the manual on being adult there's a chapter on responsibility. Maybe you should go back and re-read it."

"You really can't let go, can you?"

"It's not about letting go, Mateo. It's about all

the things that are expected of me—not least of which is taking care of you, since I'm the one who brought you here."

He reached over and brushed a stray strand of hair from her face. The feel of his hand was so startling and smooth she caught herself on the verge of recoiling, but stopped when she realized it was an empty gesture. Still, the shivers his touch left behind rattled her.

"I'm not going to let anything hurt you or your reputation," he said, his voice so low it was almost drowned out by the noise level coming from the rest of the people at The Shack. "I know how hard it is to get what you want and keep it, and I wouldn't jeopardize that for you, Lizzie."

This serious side of him…she hadn't seen it before. But she knew, deep down, this was the real Mateo coming through. Not the one who refused treatment, not even the one who partied hard on the beach. Those might be different sides to his personality, but she'd just been touched by the real Mateo Sanchez, and she liked it. Maybe for the first time liked *him*. If only she could see more of him, now.

"I appreciate that," she said.

She toyed with the idea of telling him that her job here might not be everything she wanted, that she was rethinking staying. But he didn't want to hear that. It was her dilemma to solve.

"Just keep it reasonable and we'll both be fine."

"Everything in my life has been reasonable, Lizzie. I may not remember all about that life, but I do recall who I was in the part I remember, and I was you—always too serious, always too involved."

"And now?" she asked.

"That is the question, isn't it? I have so many different pieces of me rattling around my brain, and I'm not able to put them in order yet."

And she suspected he was afraid of what he might find when he did put them into place. She understood that. Understood Mateo more now than she had.

"Sometimes they don't always come together the way you want or expect."

"Then I'll have a lifetime to adjust to what I'm missing, or what got away from me. And that's not me being pragmatic. That's me trying to deal with *me*, and I'm not easy. I know that."

He reached out and brushed her cheek, this time without the pretense of brushing back her hair. It was simply a stroke of affection or friendship. Maybe an old habit returning. And she didn't mind so much.

Affection had never really been part of her life. Not from her dad, not from her husband. Even if this little gesture from Mateo meant nothing to him, it meant something to her. But she wouldn't allow herself to think beyond that. What was the point? He was a man without a memory; she a woman without clear direction. It wasn't a good combination, no matter how you looked at it.

Still, his touch gave her the shivers again.

"So, moving on to something less philosophical, you wouldn't happen to know if I can swim, would you? I mean, being in the Army, I'm assuming I have basic skills. But enough to get me out there on one of those surfboards?"

"I could always throw you in to find out."

"You're not a very sympathetic doctor, Dr. Peterson."

She laughed. "Well, you're finally catching on."

"What I'm catching on to is that you're a

fraud. I know there's a side of Lizzie Peterson she doesn't let out. That's the side I want to see."

"Good luck with that," she said, giving his shoulder a squeeze. "Because what you see with me is what you get."

"Under different circumstances that might not be so bad. But with what I'm going through…" Mateo shrugged. "As they say: timing is everything. Too bad that's the way it's working out."

Which meant what? Was he really interested, or was this only one small aspect of Mateo that had been damaged?

"In my experience, it's not so much about the timing as it is the luck of the draw. Things happen when they happen, and the only thing dictating that is what you're doing in the moment. If I'm the one paddling around in the surf after I've been warned there's a rip current, it should come as no surprise to me that I'm also the one who gets carried out to sea. Things happen because we make them happen—or we choose to ignore what could happen in their place."

"Like my amnesia. It happened because… Well, if I knew the answer to that, I'd tell you. But my doc prefers I make the discovery on my own. 'Vulnerable mind syndrome,' he calls it. Which means my mind is open and susceptible to anything."

"Except doing the things you're supposed to in order to help yourself improve."

"Claiming amnesia on that one," he said, smiling.

"As long as you're just claiming and not believing. And as for swimming… I don't know. But at some point, after I return from my holiday, if you're still here…"

"Ah, the veiled threat."

"Not a threat. An offer to take you out and see how you do in the water."

"That could motivate me to be on my best behavior."

"Or you could motivate yourself. Your choice, Mateo. So, are you up for a wade?" she asked.

"Didn't you just say something about throwing me in?"

"Maybe I did…maybe I didn't," she teased.

Mateo laughed, then suddenly turned serious. "What happens if the real me comes back, Lizzie—all of me—and I don't like who I am?"

"You haven't given yourself enough time. And maybe you underestimate yourself. Whatever the case, you're aware of changes and that's the first step. Always be mindful of that and you'll be fine. I mean, we all lose track of ourselves at one time or another, with or without amnesia. I really believe you're more in touch with who you are than you're ready to admit. So, like I said, there's no rush. Now, if you go in the water with me, it's ankle-deep or nothing."

"I could have been a Navy SEAL...which means I'm an expert swimmer." He kicked off his flip-flops and waded out in the water with her.

"Except you were an Army surgeon, stationed in a field hospital in Afghanistan. No swimming there."

"In my mind I was doing something more glamorous and heroic."

"You *were* doing something heroic. Patching, stitching, amputating..." She took hold of his hand, even though he was in perfect physical condition, and they waded in up to their knees. "Might not have been glamorous, but you were saving lives."

"Only some of which I remember," he said, taking the lead and then pulling Lizzie along until they were in halfway to their hips.

They stood there together for a few minutes, simply looking out over the water. In the distance, a freighter was making its slow way across the horizon—not destined for Oahu, where they were, but perhaps one of the other islands.

Faraway places, she thought, as she reluctantly turned back toward shore. She'd spent her life in faraway places, but she'd never taken the time to notice as she'd been too young, or too involved in trying to get along in yet another new place.

A big pity, that. So many opportunities wasted. Maybe someday she'd go back and have a do-over. Or maybe she wouldn't. Maybe she'd put the past behind her, find her roots, and venture out to see if a little happiness might go with that. Right now, she didn't know what she'd do. Her life was a toss-up.

* * *

"You're drunk," Lizzie said, not happy about this at all. Well, maybe not downright drunk so much as a little tipsy. But it would be the same once Janis found out.

After their wade in the ocean Mateo had decided to go back and join the partiers.

"That's why I'm taking you in the back door of Makalapua. Because if we go in the front, I'll lose my job."

Actually, she wouldn't. She was the primary care physician there and that brought some clout with it. And the patients weren't prisoners. Doing what Mateo had done, while not advisable, wasn't illegal, and in the hospital not even punishable. His condition wasn't physical. He was on no medications that had any bearing on the beers he'd consumed. So nothing precluded alcohol.

Lizzie recalled the evenings when her dad had been a patient here, and she'd taken him to The Shack for tropical drink. He'd loved that. When he was lucid, he'd claimed it made him feel normal. But he hadn't been on the verge of being sent elsewhere, the way Mateo was.

Still, there was no reason for Mateo to make

a spectacle of himself—which he had done after three craft beers. He'd danced. On a table. With a waitress.

She'd turned her back to order herself another lemonade, and when she'd turned around there he'd been, doing everything a head trauma patient shouldn't do. And he'd refused to stop when she'd asked him to get off the table. It was almost like he was trying to get himself kicked out of his spot at the hospital.

It had taken two strong *wahines he'e nalu*—surfer women—to pull him down for her, and by that time he'd been so unsteady he hadn't even been able to take ten steps back without zigging and zagging. And there she'd been, looking like a total idiot, trying to get the man who'd become the life of the party to quit.

Well, in another day she'd have two whole weeks to sleep, swim, and forget about her patients, her obligations…and Mateo. Except he worried her. After having such a nice chat with him… Well, she wasn't sure what she'd hoped for, but this wasn't it.

"Not drunk. Just pleasantly mellow. And I'll take responsibility for my actions," he said, slumping in the wheelchair one of The Shack patrons had run back to the hospital and re-trieved for her.

."You bet you will—because what you did is way out of line and I'm not going to get myself into trouble because you can't control yourself."

"Meaning you're going to report me?

"Meaning I'm going to make a note in your chart. You're already close to the edge, Mateo, and you know that. Depending on what kind of mood Janis is in when she reads what I'm about to write, there's a strong likelihood she'll have you transferred. You know the policy."

"Yeah…one month to show I'm working, eight weeks to show progress. Well, isn't danc-ing progress?"

"I was trying to be nice by giving you a little time away from the hospital, but you turned it into a mess. And while dancing may show *some* sort of progress…on a table? With a wait-ress?"

"You're sounding a little jealous, Lizzie. I'd have asked you to dance, but, well…all work, no play. You'd have turned me down."

Yes, she would have. But was he right about her jealousy? Not over the other woman, but over taking the chance to have a little fun. She was all work, wasn't she? Maybe all these years of no play had caught up to her and she didn't know how to have fun. Or maybe "Daddy's little soldier," as he'd used to call her, had never known what fun was.

Lizzie pushed Mateo's wheelchair up a side hall, through the corridor behind the kitchen, then through the physical therapy storage area. Finally, when they came to the hall that led to his room, Lizzie stopped, looked around, then gave his chair a shove and stood there watching him roll away while she did nothing to stop him.

It took Mateo several seconds to realize she wasn't controlling him, and by the time he'd taken hold of the chair wheels he was sitting in the middle of the hall, too woozy to push himself past the two rooms before his.

"Why are you doing this to me?" he asked, managing to move himself along, but very slowly.

"That's the same question I was asking just a little while ago," she said, walking behind him. "Why are you putting me in this position?"

"Maybe there's something wrong with my

amygdala or even my anterior cingulate cortex. You know—the areas that affect impulse control and decision-making."

"Your brain is fine. I've seen enough CTs of it to know there's nothing wrong. The blood clot was removed successfully. No other bruising or swelling present. No tumors. No unexplained shadows. So you've got no physical excuse for the way you act."

When they came to the door to his room Mateo maneuvered to turn in, didn't make it, backed away, and tried again, this time scraping the frame as he entered.

"I wasn't aware I was putting you in any kind of bad position," he said, stopping short of the bed and not trying to get out of his chair.

"Seriously? You don't work, you don't co-operate with the nurses, you refuse to go to your cognitive therapy sessions most of the time, and when you do go you don't stay long. You've recovered from a traumatic brain injury and you're battling retrograde amnesia, Mateo, in case you've forgotten. Then you get drunk and dance on a table. All that puts me in a very difficult position."

She had no idea if he was even listening to

her. His eyes were staring out of the window and there was no expression on his face to tell her anything.

"Look, I like you. And I know you're in a tough spot—you look normal, but you're not normal enough to get back to your old life."

"My old life?" he said finally, and his voice was starting to fill with anger. "You mean the one where I was a surgeon one minute and then, in the blink of an eye, a surgeon's patient? Is that what you're calling 'a tough spot?' And don't tell me how I'm working my way through the five stages of grief and I'm stuck on anger, because I damn well *know* that. What I don't know is what happened to me, or why, or what I was doing prior to the accident, or anything I did last year. And I'd say that's a hell of a lot more than *a tough spot*."

He shook his head, but still didn't turn to face her.

"I'm sorry if I got you in trouble. That wasn't my intention. Being a bad patient isn't my intention either. But when you don't know..." He swallowed hard. "When you don't know who you are anymore, strange things happen in your mind. Maybe you were this...maybe you were that. Maybe you're not even close to who you were. I have a lot of memories, Lizzie, and I'm thankful for that. But sometimes, when I'm confronted with something I should know, and it's not there…"

"It scares you?"

"To death."

"My dad… I lived for three years with him, watching him go through that same tough spot and never returning from it. His life was taken from him in bits and pieces until there were more gaps than memories—and he knew that. At least until he didn't know anything anymore. He didn't have the option of moving on, starting over in a life that, while it wasn't his, was still a good life. There's going to come a time when you must move on with whatever you have left and be glad you have that option. Some people don't."

She walked over to him, laid a reassuring hand on his shoulder, and gave him a squeeze.

"You've got to cooperate with your doctors, Mateo, instead of working against them. Right now, working against them is all you do, and I'm willing to bet that's not the way you were before the accident."

"I'd tell you if I knew," he said, his voice more sad now than angry. "I'm sorry about your dad, Lizzie. He deserved better. Anyway, my head is spinning and all I want to do is sleep. But I think I'll need some help out of the chair."

Immediately alert, Lizzie pulled a penlight from her pocket and bent over him to look into his eyes, in case there was something else going on with him other than the beginnings of a hangover.

"Look up," she said. "Now, down…to the right…to the left."

When she saw nothing of note, she tucked away her light, then offered Mateo a hand to help him get up. Which he did—but too fast. He wavered for a moment, then pitched forward into Lizzie's arms.

"Care to dance *now*?" he asked, not even trying to push himself away.

Admittedly, he felt good. And she could smell a faint trace of aftershave, even though he typically sported a three-day-old stubble. Had he splashed on a dash of scent for their walk?

"I think you've already done enough of that," she said, guiding him to the bed.

Once he was sitting, she helped him lift his legs, then removed his flip-flops when he was stretched out on the bed.

"I'll have one of the nurses come in and help you change into your..."

There was no point in continuing. Mateo was already out. Dead to the world. Sleeping like a baby.

And she—well...time to face Janis.

This wasn't how this part of her day was supposed to have gone. Taking a patient out for a walk...him getting drunk...

Thank heavens she had two blissful weeks of sitting on the beach, reading, and swimming coming up. She needed the rest. Needed to be away from her responsibilities. Needed to put her own life in order in so many ways.

# CHAPTER THREE

"No, it's not your fault," Janis said, handing Lizzie a tiki cup filled with a Hawaiian Twist—a drink made of banana, pineapple, and coconut milk. And, yes, she'd even put a paper umbrella in it—not that Lizzie needed a tiki cup, a paper umbrella, or even a Hawaiian Twist. But Janis loved to make island favorites for anybody who came to her office, and today this was the favorite.

So Lizzie took a drink and, amazingly, it made her feel a little bit better. It didn't ease the headache, but it gave her a mental boost.

"It's not like I haven't taken a patient out for a walk before."

"Well, that's why we built the hospital here," Janis said, sitting down in a wicker chair across from Lizzie.

They were on the lanai outside Janis's office, as a perfect tropical breeze swept in around them.

"I know—to take advantage of the location.

And the gardens. Because we want our patients to experience paradise. And I do truly believe there are curative powers in simply sitting and enjoying the view. And, in the case of some of our patients, when the memory is gone, they can still find beauty in the moment."

"Sometimes you're too soft," Janis said. "It's not necessarily a bad thing, considering most of the patients we treat, but for Mateo I'm not sure it's a good thing. He's a strong man, with a strong will, and right now that will isn't working to his advantage. I think he's trying to find his way around it. Get a foothold somewhere. Honestly, there's something in Mateo that just isn't clicking."

"Do you think he's trying to take advantage of me? Hoping I can do something for him?"

"He could be. It's always a consideration with some of our patients."

"Well, he seems harmless enough to me. And it's not like anything is going to happen between us."

"Just be careful of Mateo. I haven't figured him out yet."

"Nothing's going on," Lizzie stated. "We've crossed paths for weeks, and this evening I just… It was a *walk*, Janis. That's all. Except for the drinking, everything was fine."

"Everything except you gave in to your sentimental side and he used it against you. Be careful, Lizzie. I've seen it happen before and it never turns out well. And you're better than that."

Janis was right. She *was* better than that. But it wasn't showing right now. Yet she wasn't sure that she wouldn't take another walk with Mateo if he suggested it. Why? Because he was attractive? Because when the real man shone through she liked him? Because she was in the middle of her own crisis and Mateo was a distraction?

"Why don't you go ahead and start your holiday early? Get away from here. Forget us, forget your patients, and most of all, forget Mateo."

"There's no one to cover for me."

"The locum arrives in the morning. We'll put him straight to work while you sleep in or sip a mimosa on your lanai. However you choose to spend your days off, Lizzie, they start tomorrow. I need you back at your best and, while I have no complaints about your work, you seem so distant lately. Take the time…get it sorted."

Forget Mateo? Easier said than done. But with any luck, and two weeks of rest ahead of her, she'd get much more sorted than Mateo. Her dad. Her life. Putting things into perspective.

Now, that was something she was looking forward to.

In her life she worked, she slept, and every Saturday morning she went surfing, if conditions were right. That was it. All of it. And even though she owned her house she'd never really settled in, because she had been so up in the air about her dad.

Was this the place for him? Did he have the best caregiver? Did he need more? Should she enroll him in a day program a few times a week even though he wouldn't have a clue what it was about?

She'd taken care of her dad for five years before he died, and all her energies outside work had been devoted to him.

Of course, she'd been contacted about great facilities all over the country that would have taken him in and made his last days meaningful. But what would have been "meaning-ful" to him? Her voice? The familiarity of his old trinkets and clothes? The chicken and rice she'd fixed him every Saturday night that he'd seemed to enjoy, when his enjoyment of other foods had gone away?

He'd had so little left, and there had been nothing any of these facilities could have done to make him better, so why deprive him of things he might remember?

Which was why she was here. He'd always wanted to retire to Hawaii and spend his days sitting on the beach, or planting flowers. That was what she'd given him when they'd moved here…the last thing she could recall that he'd ever asked for.

Now, here she still was, not sure whether to stay and live with the memories or go and start over someplace else. She really didn't have a life here. All her time had been taken up by work or her dad. Then, after he'd died, she'd filled in the empty hours with more work. Now it was all she could see for herself, and she wasn't sure she liked what she saw.

So maybe it was finally time to settle down, turn her house into a home, and start working on some of those plans she'd made when she'd moved here.

"I'll call you in a few days and let you know how it's going," she said to Janis as she headed out the door. "And maybe I'll have a party. A vegetarian luau."

"With lots of rum punch, since they won't be getting roast pig?"

Lizzie laughed. "Sounds like a plan. And if you get swamped, let me know. I'll come back."

"I know you will—which is why I'm going to ban you from the hospital until you're back to work full-time. Understand?"

Janis could be hard. In her position she had to be. But, as her former med school professor, and now her friend, she was the best. In fact, she'd been the one who'd offered to take her dad, when his Alzheimer's had been on the verge of becoming unmanageable at home. She'd even come to the mainland to help her make the move.

"Then how about we meet up at The Shack every few days and you can tell me all the gossip?" Lizzie suggested.

"Or maybe you could hang around there by

yourself…meet a man…preferably a nice blond surf bum. How long's it been since…?"

"*Too* long," Lizzie said. "For anything. No details necessary."

"Then definitely find yourself a surf bum. A nice one with an older brother for me."

Lizzie was thirty-four, and Janis had twenty years on her, but with her blonde hair, and her teeny-bikini-worthy body, Janis was the one the men looked at while Lizzie was hiding in the shadows, taking mental notes on how to be outgoing.

"I thought you liked them younger these days?" Lizzie teased.

"I like them any way I can have them." She smiled at Lizzie. "Seriously, take care of yourself. And keep in touch."

"OK and OK," she said, then waved backward as she walked away, intending to head back to her office, tidy up, then leave.

But before she got there she took a detour and headed down the wrong hall. Or the right one, if her destination was Mateo's room. Which, this evening, it was.

"Well, the good news is I get to start my holiday early," she said to Matteo, who was sitting in a chair next to the window, simply looking out over the evening shadows of the garden, and not sound asleep in bed, as she'd expected. "So, this is me telling you goodbye and good luck."

"What? No more dates at The Shack?"

"First one was a total bust. With me it's one strike and you're out."

"But you haven't seen the real me. When that Mateo Sanchez emerges, do I get another chance?"

Lizzie laughed. "I'm betting you were a real charmer with the ladies. One look into those dark eyes and…"

"Do *you* like my eyes?" he interrupted.

She did—more than she should—and she'd almost slipped up there.

"Eyes are eyes. They're nice to use to get a clear picture of when you're being played."

"I'm not playing you, Lizzie."

"It doesn't matter if you are or you aren't. I'm off on holiday now, and once I'm outside the hospital door everything here will be forgotten for two whole weeks."

"Including me, Lizzie?"

"Especially you, Mateo. So, if you're not here when I return…have a good life."

He stood, then crossed the room to her before she could get out the door. He pulled her into his arms. He nudged her chin up with his thumb and simply stared into her eyes for a moment. But then sense and logic overtook him and he broke his hold on her and stepped away.

"We can't do this," he whispered. "I want to so badly, but I never should have started this, and I'm sorry."

"So am I," she said, backing all the way out through the door, and trying to walk to the hospital exit without showing off her wobbly knees.

Whatever had just happened couldn't happen again. She wasn't ready. Her life was in a mess. But it was one more thing to be sorted in her time off.

Was she really beginning to develop feelings for Mateo?

Or was Janis right?

Was he looking for a foothold? Someone to use?

*Was he playing her?*

She didn't want to believe that, but the thought was there. And so was the idea that she had to shore up her reserves to resist him, because he wasn't going to make it easy.

He wasn't sure what to think. Didn't even know if he cared. Still, what he'd done was stupid. Going against hospital policy. Drinking a little too much, dancing to prove…well, he wasn't sure what he had been trying to prove.

Had he been the doctor of a patient like himself he'd have taken it much worse than Janis and Randy had. In fact, all things considered, they'd been very calm. Or was it the calm before the storm?

Lizzie wasn't here to defend him now, and he missed her. Not just because she'd seemed to take his side, but because he genuinely liked her. Maybe even missed her already. Right now, he didn't have any friends, and she'd turned out to be not only a friend but someone he trusted.

Except she wasn't in the picture now. He was on his own and trying to figure out what would come next in his life.

"None of this is what I planned," he said aloud to himself as he looked out the window.

Five years in the military, then find a good surgical practice somewhere in a mountainous area. Or maybe near canyons or desert. He wasn't quite sure what he'd wanted, to be honest, but those were the areas that were tugging on his mind, so maybe that was what he'd wanted pre-amnesia. Not that it mattered now.

"You haven't been to your cognitive therapy group," Randy Jenkins said from the doorway.

He was a short man with thick glasses, who wore dress pants and a blue shirt, a tie and a white lab coat. He didn't look like he'd seen the inside of a smile in a decade.

"Haven't even left your room. You're way past the point where your meals should be served to you on a tray in your room. But you're refusing to come to the dining room."

Because he didn't want to. Because nothing here was helping him. Because he wanted his old life back, whatever that was, and he was pretty sure it didn't involve sitting in a group with nine other memory loss patients talking about things they didn't remember.

"And what, exactly, will those prescribed

things do for me?" he asked, turning to face the man.

"Give you a sense of where you are now, since you can't go back to where you were before."

"Where I am now is looking out a window at a life that isn't mine."

"Do you *want* to get better, Doctor?"

Mateo shook his head angrily. "What I want is what I can't have. And that's something you can't fix."

"But there are other things you can do besides be a surgeon."

"And how do you think I should address the obvious in my curriculum vitae? *Unemployed surgeon with amnesia looking for work*?"

It wasn't Randy's fault. He knew that. It wasn't anybody's fault. But he was so empty right now. Empty, and afraid to face the future without all his memories of the past.

"Look, sit in on a therapy session this afternoon. Then come for your private session with me. I'll have my assistant look for some training programs that might interest you and—"

"Training programs? Don't you understand? I'm a surgeon."

"No, you're not. Not anymore. I've had to report you to the medical licensing board and—"

"You couldn't have waited until we were a little farther along in this?"

"You're not *in* this, Mateo. And that's the problem. Your license as a surgeon will be provisionally suspended, pending review and recommendations if and when you recover. I had to do it or risk my own medical license."

He'd worked so hard to get that. Spent years and more money than he'd had. Even if he couldn't operate, at least he had the license that proved he'd achieved his lifelong goal. He'd been somebody. But now he didn't even have that.

"I guess we all do what we have to do, don't we?" he said.

"It's nothing personal. And, for what it's worth, you'll probably still have your general license to practice, because at the end of all this there's every likelihood you'll be able to find a place in medicine, somewhere. But you've got to cooperate *now*."

But if he cooperated that meant all this was real. And he wasn't ready for that yet. Which was why he fought so hard against everything.

Once he admitted it was real, he was done. Over. Nothing to hope for. Nothing left to hold on to. Not even that thin scrap of resistance.

Two days had gone by and she was already feeling better. She'd boxed up a few of her dad's belongings, which she'd been putting off for too long. Read a book on the history of Kamehameha, which had been sitting dusty on her shelf for two years. Done a bit of surfing and swimming.

Even just two days had done her a world of good, and as she headed off to the little stretch of beach at the front of her house, a guava and passionfruit drink in her hand, she was looking forward to more relaxation, more time to figure out if she should stay here or go somewhere else and start over.

Her plan had always been to go back home to upstate New York, but little by little this tiny patch of land she owned on Oahu had drawn her in. Her house was all glass on the side with the ocean view. It was large, but not too large...comfortable. Her dad had planted flowers that still bloomed in the garden and would for years to come, and the thought of leaving those brought a lump to her throat because he'd loved them so much in the last good days of his memory.

Her job… Well, that was one of those things she needed to rethink. It was good, but she wasn't sure it was where she belonged. She liked working there, loved working with Janis, but the whole fit seemed…*off*. Maybe because her dad was gone now. Maybe because she was alone. Or maybe those thoughts were simply her fatigue taking over. And, since she wasn't one to make rash decisions, she was going to let the job situation ride. Work through to the end of her contract, then see how she was feeling.

Stretching out on a lounger, Lizzie sat her drink on a little table topped with a mosaic of beach shells that her dad had collected and let her gaze drift to the waves lapping her small beach. She owned a *beach*. An honest-to-goodness beach. Even the sound of it impressed her a little, when very little else did these days.

"It's a nice view," came a familiar voice from behind her.

"How did you know where to find me?" she asked, turning to see Mateo standing just a few feet away with a duffle bag slung casually over his shoulder.

"Went to The Shack. Asked. They knew you and pointed me in the right direction."

"So, I'm assuming that since you've got your duffel you're no longer a patient?"

"Randy Jenkins made the recommendation this morning that I be transferred and your friend Janis dropped the axe." He shrugged. "So here I am."

"Then you're on your way to another facility?"

Mateo shook his head. "My transfer is back to California, where I was before I came here. It didn't do me any good then, and nothing's changed so it's not going to do me any good now."

This wasn't good. Too many soldiers returned home with PTSD and other problems and ended up on the street. Suddenly, she feared that for Mateo.

"What are your plans?" she asked, not sure she wanted to hear them.

"Don't have any. When they said they'd arrange a transfer in a couple of days I arranged my own."

"Meaning you're homeless? Or do you have a home somewhere?"

She didn't want to get involved. Shouldn't get involved. But he didn't deserve this, and it wasn't his fault that he'd lost the life he'd known.

"No home. Sold it when I went into the Army and used the proceeds to buy a house for my mother. It's in Mexico, and I'm not a citizen there. To get my veterans' medical benefits I have to live in the States. Meaning until I leave Hawaii I'm a beach bum. But before I take off to…let's call it to 'discover myself,' I wanted to thank you for being so kind to me and trying to help. I appreciate your efforts, Dr. Elizabeth Peterson, even if they were wasted."

"And what now? You walk off into the sunset? Because that's not where you're going to find yourself, Mateo."

He shrugged. "Do you really think I'll find myself if I'm admitted to an eight-bed ward and assigned to therapy to which I won't go, until I'm deemed so uncooperative they put me away in a home, give me drugs, and let me spend the rest of my life shuffling through the halls wearing bedroom slippers and existing in some kind of a stupor?"

"It's not that bad," she argued, even though she knew that in some cases it could be.

But for Mateo…she didn't know. He wanted something he wouldn't get back and he was stuck in the whole denial process. For how long, she had no clue. She was a personal care physician, not a psychiatrist.

"Could you go stay with your mother for a while?"

"I could, but she still doesn't know what happened to me and I'd rather keep it that way as long as I can."

"Well, I admire the reason, but how long do you intend on keeping up the charade?"

"To be honest, I don't know. Haven't thought it through that far, yet."

Everything inside Lizzie was screaming not to get involved, that Mateo wasn't her problem. But she felt involvement creeping up, pulling her toward the edge.

She thought of that day her dad had wandered off, just a year ago. If only someone had found him in time… And while Mateo wasn't at all in the same condition there could be just as many bad consequences for him as well. So, swallowing hard as she pushed aside all the reasons why she shouldn't do it, she did it anyway.

"Look, there's an *ohana* unit on the other side of the house. It's small, but no one's using it, and you're welcome to stay there a couple of days until you get things sorted."

"This is where me and my bad attitude would usually take offense or say something to make you angry or hurt your feelings, but I'm not going to do that. I didn't come here looking for help, but I'm grateful you're offering. So, yes, I'd appreciate staying in your *ohana*. Because I don't want to be out there wandering alone, trying to find something I might not even recognize. I don't like being this way, Lizzie. Don't like being uncooperative…don't like hearing half the things I'm saying. But if I do get to be too much for you to handle, kick me out. You deserve better than what I know I'm capable of doing."

"I don't suppose you can cook?" she asked.

He chuckled. "No clue. But if you're willing to take a chance with an amnesiac surgeon in your kitchen…"

\* \* \*

*For the past two days there had been nothing incoming, meaning nothing outgoing either. No imposed time limit on life or death. One less death to record, one less chopped-up body to send back was always good.*

*Passing the time playing cards with his best buddy Freddy wasn't necessarily what he wanted to be doing, but there wasn't anything else. And it was always interesting to see the many ways Freddy cheated at cards. Some Mateo caught. Many he did not. He could see it—Freddy palming one card and trading it for another.*

*"Cheat," he accused his friend. All in fun, though.*

*"Prove it," Freddy always said. "Prove it, and when we get back I'll buy you the best steak dinner you'll ever eat."*

*Problem was Mateo couldn't prove it. Freddy was just as slick in his card-playing skills as he was at being a medic. The plan was that after they returned home Freddy would finish medical school and eventually end up as Mateo's partner.*

*But tonight, there was no plan, and Freddy*

*was pacing the hall the way he did when he got notice that someone was on their way in. In those tense minutes just before everything changed. Activity doubled. The less injured soldiers stepped aside for the more injured.*

*Sometimes they lined up in tribute, saluting as the medical team rushed through the door, pushing a gurney carrying the latest casualty.*

*"Stop it!" Mateo shouted at his friend. "Don't do that! Because if you do they'll come. Stop it. Do you hear me? Stop it!"*

*But Freddy kept on pacing, waiting...*

*No, not tonight. Mateo wanted to make it three nights in a row without a casualty.*

*"One more night. Just one more night..."*

Outside in the back garden, on her way to take fresh towels and linens to the *ohana*, Lizzie stood quietly at his door, listening. He'd excused himself to take a nap while she'd stayed on the beach to read. Now this.

It hadn't happened in the rehab center, but something here was triggering it. Perhaps getting close to someone again? Close to her?

She thought about going in and waking him up. Then decided against it. If he was working out his demons in his sleep, he needed to. Besides, he was here as a friend, not a patient, and she had to take off her doctor persona or this would never work.

But it worried her. Because she knew the end of the story. Mateo's best friend had been killed in the raid that had injured him. Mateo had been pulled from the carnage and taken to the hospital, resisting help because he'd wanted to go back to save his friend. Except his best friend couldn't be saved.

While she wasn't a neurologist, she wondered if some deep, buried grief over that was contributing to his condition. Certainly the head injury was. But not being able to save his friend…? She understood that profoundly. Because in the end she hadn't been able to save her father. It was a guilt that consumed her every day.

"Sleep well?" she asked, watching Mateo come through the door. Cargo shorts, T-shirt, mussed hair. She liked dark hair. Actually, she had never really thought about what she liked in terms of the physical aspects of a man, but she knew she liked the physical aspects of Mateo. Strong, muscled...

"Bed's comfortable, but I don't feel rested. Guess I've got more sleep to catch up on than I thought."

Sleep without nightmares, she thought.

"Well, the folks at Makalapua weren't happy to find out where you are. Apparently, you got out of their transportation at the end of the circular drive, when the driver stopped to enter the main road, and then disappeared."

"Transportation? Is that what they call it?"

"Makalapua owns a limo for transporting patients and families when necessary."

"And it also owns an ambulance, Lizzie. *That* was my transportation. Ordered by my doctor. They came in with a gurney, strapped me down to it, and shoved me in the back of the ambulance. I was leaving as a *patient*. Not a guest. And I'm tired of being a patient."

Lizzie sat down on the rattan armchair in her living room and gripped the armrests. "An ambulance? I don't believe—"

"I may have amnesia," he interrupted, "but I still remember what a gurney and an ambulance are. Oh, and in case you didn't hear,

I was to be escorted straight onto a military medical plane and met at the airport in California—probably with a gurney and an ambulance there, too."

"Did you get violent? Is that why they did it?"

"Mad as hell, but not violent." He sat down on the two-cushion sofa across from her but kept to the edge of it. "I'm guessing a couple of them are mad as hell right now."

"They only want to help you, Mateo."

*They only want to help you.*

*We only want to help you.*

*I only want to help you.*

Words she'd said over and over for years. Before, they'd sounded perfectly fine. Now, they sounded deceitful.

"Well, restraining me rather than giving me a sedative was preferable, but they were sending me to the place I specifically asked not to be sent."

"You're still Army, Mateo. On inactive duty. That means your commanders make the call and—"

"It's out of my hands." He shook his head

in frustration. "I'm theirs until they cut me loose."

"Something like that. And you knew that's how it would be when you went in. When the military and veterans' hospitals didn't work for you, you were given a chance to recover outside the normal system. So, from what I'm seeing, they really were trying to help."

And now he was in no system but, instead in her *ohana*.

"Look, let me see if I can work something out with Janis. Maybe we can get you transferred somewhere else. Maybe another private hospital."

"Or maybe I should just go grab my things and wander on down the beach. The weather's nice. A lot of people move from their homes to the beaches during the hottest weather. Maybe someone will take pity on me and give me a meal every now and then."

"You're not going to live on the beach, Mateo. And I'm not sending you off on some journey to search for something you might not even remember when you find it."

Visions of her dad getting out and wandering around alone were the essence of her nightmares. And she'd even had a live-in caregiver who hadn't always been able to keep track of him.

"So for now you stay here, and we'll see what we can figure out."

"But the military…they know where I am?" he asked.

"Of course they do. I called them because you're not free of your obligation and they had to know. Like I've told you before, I play by the rules. But they're not going to come and take you away from here, Mateo. At least not yet. All they wanted was to know where you were and what you were doing. I told them you were going into outpatient care in a few days."

"That's what you think I'm going to do?"

"That's what I *know* you're going to do if you want to stay here. Janis approved it and, for the record, it's your last chance. After this the Army takes you back, and they'll be the only ones with a say in what happens."

Finally, he relaxed back into the sofa. "These last weeks it's like someone's always doing something to me, and most of the time not even consulting me before they do it. You're the first one who's ever told me beforehand what would happen, and I appreciate that."

"So…you mentioned your mother doesn't know about your current condition? Why is that? Is there some way she could take over medical responsibility for you until you're through this?"

He shook his head adamantly. "She has advanced diabetes. Arthritis. Partially blind. The less she knows, the better off she is. Like I said before, I do call her every day, and as soon as I'm free to travel I'll go to see her. But I don't want the stress of knowing what I'm going through anywhere near her. She deserves a better life than she's ever had before and I'm not going to deprive her of that."

"Which makes you a very good son."

She recalled how, in her dad's decline, she'd tried to keep so many things away from him— things that would cause him stress. So she certainly understood what Mateo was doing, and even admired him for that. It wasn't easy. She knew that.

"I remember when my mother became a citizen in the US. She'd studied for weeks, worked hard to learn the history, the language, and I think the day she was sworn in was one of the proudest days of her life. Making a new life isn't easy, and she did it for me."

"And you?"

"I was too young to realize all the sacrifices she was making to give me a better life. I don't think I appreciated it the way I should. And my mother... I don't want her worrying about me. It's the least I can do. And she's happy back in Mexico, living near her sister, proud of her son the...the doctor." He nearly choked on the words.

She thought about the life her dad had made for her. That had never been easy either, but it had always been good. And he'd put aside many opportunities because he'd chosen to be a father first.

"Anyway, what's next, Mateo? What do you want to happen or expect to happen?"

He chuckled, but bitterly. "Look, Lizzie. I don't know what I'm doing, and I'm sure that's obvious. But I'm not going to impose, and I'm not going to expect you to be my doctor while I'm here."

"Like I *could* be your doctor," she said.

"That would require ethical considerations I don't want to think about. Doctor brings patient home for special treatment? Nope, not me. I can be your friend, even a medical colleague, but not your doctor. So, my friend, I want to take a walk down to The Shack and ask them why they thought it was appropriate to tell someone where I live."

"Then what?" he asked.

"Then guilt them into free shrimp burgers. They're *so* good. But no beer. And no dancing on the table."

"In my defense, it was only a couple feet off the ground."

"You have no defense, Mateo. Absolutely none. And if I catch you up on a table, and I don't care how high it is…" She pointed to the chaise on the lanai. "*That's* as far as you'll go. I might toss you a pillow and a plate of food every now and then, but if you dance on a table I'm done."

Mateo laughed. "You know, from the first moment I saw you walk by my hospital room I knew you were a real softie. Your threats don't scare me, Lizzie. You haven't got it in you to make me sleep out there."

Unfortunately, that was true. Something about Mateo caused her usual resolve to simply melt away.

It wasn't like him to think only in the moment. At least, he didn't *think* it was like him. He'd looked at his calendar and seen that he'd made notes about plans well into the future. Some things still months away. That was certainly a personality trait he didn't remember—especially now, when he was basically on the edge of living rough and not particularly worried about it.

Was that because he knew he could count on Lizzie as his backup?

Mateo looked at his half-eaten shrimp burger and wondered if he even liked shrimp. Had he been allergic his throat would have swollen shut by now. He might even be dead. But he wasn't, and his throat was fine.

Subconsciously, he raised his hand to his throat and rubbed it.

"You OK?" Lizzie asked him.

She was sitting across from him at a high-top

for two, looking like an Irish lassie who simply fitted in here. Red hair wild. Brown eyes sparkling with gold flecks that were highlighted by the glow of the citronella candle on their table. The brightest, widest smile he'd ever seen.

"Just wondering if I have allergies."

"According to your military records, you don't."

"You really know more about me than I know about myself, don't you?" he asked. Realizing she had access to his life while he didn't felt strange.

"You do understand why I don't just tell you everything I know, don't you?"

"So you won't fill my impressionable mind with fake notions of who I am. I know it would be easy…false memories and all that. But sitting here with a stranger who knows me inside and out, while only a couple of hours ago I was homeless without a plan is…disconcerting."

Lizzie reached across the table and squeezed his hand. "I'll bet it is. But if you ever settle down you'll work through some of it. Maybe even more than you expect."

He studied her hand for a moment— porcelain-smooth skin, a little on the pale side compared to most of the people at The Shack. Nice hand. Gentle.

"Now that you're not restricted by any kind of medical ethics with me, tell me how much I can expect to return. Or how much will never return. Can you do that much for me?"

She pulled her hand back. "There's no formula for that, Mateo. No way to predict. I'd like to be able to give you a definitive answer, but the brain can't be predicted. You may be where you're always going to be now, or you may improve. Losing pieces of yourself—or, as I call it, living in a fog—has got to be difficult. I see it, and I understand it, but I can't relate to it."

He smiled. "Wish I couldn't relate to it either. Look, I appreciate you taking me in for a couple of days. I really do need some time to figure out what comes next. But you're not responsible for me, Lizzie. Just be patient for a little while, and on my end of it I promise no more dancing on the table or anything else. I'll be cooperative. Tell me what to do and I'll do it."

He meant it, too. It was time to figure out his life, and it was nice having a friend on his side to help him. A friend who was patient and caring the way Lizzie was.

"Why didn't you do that at the hospital?"

"Four walls, a bed, and a window to the world. That's all it was, and it scared me, Lizzie. Still does when I think that's all my life might be about."

"So you refuse traditional help, do everything you can to distance yourself from it, in order to—what? I want to know, Mateo. If I hadn't lived within walking distance of the hospital, or if a couple of the people who work here hadn't known where I live, what would you have done? Because so far all you've done is walk away. From Germany, from the veterans' facility in Boston, then in California, and from the hospital here. From—"

She shut up and took a bite of her burger.

"From *everything*, Mateo," she said, once she'd swallowed. "And it all adds up to you walking away from yourself."

"You were going to say fiancée, weren't you?"

"You remember her?"

"Vaguely. Must have been a short relationship, because she didn't leave much behind in my head. Except, maybe… She didn't want to live with someone in my condition, did she?"

"Actually, I don't know the whole story. It was in your chart, but since you weren't my patient I didn't read it. The only things I know about you are what I heard at the weekly patient review meetings."

"That's right. By the book, Lizzie."

"You think that's a problem?"

"I think in today's medical world it's an asset. There are too many people getting involved in aspects of a patient's care who shouldn't."

Suddenly he could feel the tiredness coming on. And the headache. Dull to blinding in sixty seconds. So, rather than pursuing this conversation, he stood abruptly, tossed a few dollars on the table—enough to cover both meals and a tip—then walked away. He wanted to get out of there before the full force of the headache made him queasy, caused him to stagger.

Once away from The Shack, Mateo headed toward the beach, then sat down on the sand, shut his eyes, and tried to clear his head.

Right now, he didn't care about what Lizzie

was holding back. All he cared about was the pain level rising in him and how to control it.

And that didn't come easy these days. Not easy at all.

She wasn't going to interrupt him, sitting alone out there on the sand. Mateo was entitled to his moods and his mood swings and it wasn't her place to hover over him. If he needed her help, he'd ask. Or not.

It was almost an hour later when he returned to the house. When she looked in Mateo's eyes she saw how lost he was, but she also saw the depth of the man. He was in there—just locked away.

"Look, I'm going out for a night swim, then I'm going to sit on the lanai for a while to relax. You're welcome to come, or you're welcome to stay here and read a book, watch a movie—whatever you want to do."

"You don't have to feel responsible for me, Lizzie. I can take care of myself."

"I was just being polite. You look tired, and I thought a swim might make you feel better."

He looked more than tired. He looked weary. Beaten down. He looked like a man who was fighting with everything he had to get back on the right path. It worried her, even though she had no right to be worried. Still, she couldn't help herself. There was something about Mateo that simply pulled at her.

"And I was just being honest. I don't want you disrupting your life for me."

She smiled. "To be honest, I hadn't intended on doing that. I just thought it would be a nice way to end the evening."

With that she went upstairs, changed into her swimsuit—a modest one-piece, black, no frills, nothing revealing—and went straight to the beach alone, leaving Mateo watching some blathering documentary on her TV.

*Too bad*, she thought as she dipped her toe in the surf. He might have enjoyed this. And she might have enjoyed doing this with him.

She was stunning, even though she was trying to hide it in that swimsuit. But her kind of beauty couldn't be hidden. Not the outside beauty, and not the inside beauty.

This was a huge imposition, him living in her home. He knew that. But so much of him wanted to get to know her and, while ending up here really hadn't been his intention, when good fortune had smiled on him he hadn't had it in him to turn his back on it.

He moved along the beach from where Lizzie had entered the water. He wanted to join her, but he didn't want to impose. Yet he'd wandered down here, not sure what he was hoping for. Another invitation? Perhaps nothing?

In all honesty he had no right to think anything or want anything, in his condition. But watching Lizzie… It gave him hope he hadn't felt before. Maybe something in him would change. Or something would reset and at least allow him to look forward.

Unfortunately, Lizzie coming into his life now was too soon. He could see himself with her, but not yet.

Sighing, Mateo shut his eyes. All he could see was Lizzie. Her face. The way she looked at him. Sadness. Compassion. She had the power to change a man. The power to change *him*. And maybe that was good. He didn't know, but it felt right. Felt like he was ready.

She'd been on his mind constantly, and he'd thought of little else other than Lizzie from that first moment in the hospital, when she'd walked into his room, sat down in the chair opposite him and hadn't said a word. Not one single word. She had smiled as she'd watched him, but she hadn't talked, and it had got to the point that it had been so distracting, even annoying, that he'd been the one to break the silence.

"Why are you doing that?" he'd asked her.

"Sometimes you learn more from observing than talking," she'd told him.

"And what did you learn from observing me?" he'd asked.

"That you're not going to be easy for your doctors."

Mateo chuckled. Prophetic words. He hadn't been. Still wasn't. And she'd known that simply by observing him.

"There's a shorter way back to the house," Lizzie said, sitting down beside him on the rock where he'd been sitting for the past half hour.

"I didn't hear you coming." He scooted over to give her room.

"But I saw you sitting here. I used to sit here back when my dad was getting bad. I was looking for answers, and even though there were none I always went away with a sense of calm. Back then, calm was good."

"This whole area is nice. Not sure I found any calm here, but the view is amazing." He slid his hand across the rock until it was just skimming hers. "The only places I've ever lived were congested...loud."

"Sounds like a tough way to live life," Lizzie commented.

"There are a lot of tough ways to live life, Lizzie. Some we choose, some we don't." He stood. "Anyway, it's been a long, unexpected day, and I'm ready to see if I can get some more sleep. So..." He looked at her, then shrugged. "Care to have me walk you home?"

Lizzie smiled, then stood and took his arm. "I always did love a gallant man. Just never knew they existed outside of fairy-tale books."

"Well, consider me a poor and humble prince who's at your beck and call." He gave her a low-sweeping bow then extended his arm to her.

"Poor?" she asked, as they made their way along the path. "I saw your financials when you were admitted. You're not wealthy, but you're certainly not poor."

"Then maybe poor of spirit?"

Lizzie laughed. "Somehow I doubt that. I think you're a man with an abundance of spirit. It's just that your spirit is in hiding right now."

Mateo was testing her like he'd done in the hospital with everyone else he'd encountered. It was the same, but different, because now he was living in the real world, which called for real coping skills instead of avoidance.

He'd get the hang of it. She was sure of that. But what he *wouldn't* get the hang of was using her as his enabler. Once she'd enabled her dad too much for too long. In doing that she'd denied the obvious—that the next corner he turned would be worse than the one before. And the one after that worse again.

Well, not with Mateo. He was testing new legs, so to speak. Taking new steps. Learning new things to fill in the gaps. As much as she wanted to make it her battle, it wasn't. For Mateo to get better, find his new direction, he had to take those steps by himself, fight his way through to something that fit.

She could be on the sidelines, watching, maybe holding out a supporting hand. But it was his destiny to control. She had to keep telling herself that. His destiny, not hers.

But it wasn't easy walking into her house by herself, going up the steps to bed alone. No, none of it was easy. In the morning, though, depending on what Mateo did or didn't do tonight, she'd decide what she would do. Or would not do.

## CHAPTER FOUR

THE SMELL WAS HEAVENLY. Coffee and… Was something baking? Lizzie wanted to bask in bed a while longer, simply to enjoy the rich variety of aromas drifting up to her, and she could do that. Nothing was stopping her. She was on holiday, after all. She could bask, lounge, sleep, do anything she wanted.

But the clock on her phone showed it was just a few minutes until eleven, which meant she'd spent most of the morning doing that already. It was amazing how good it felt—especially with her bad sleeping habits. Never more than an hour or two at a time. Sometimes missing sleep altogether for a day or more.

Also, she wanted to see Mateo. No particular reason. She simply wanted to see him and ask what he planned for the day.

So a quick shower and Lizzie was on her way downstairs, where he was waiting for her at the bottom, holding out a coffee mug.

"There was no cream, and you don't strike me as the type who'd go in for gratuitous sugar, so it's black. But I did find a papaya tree outside and I picked a ripe one, juiced it, and added a bit to your coffee."

"You remember what a papaya is?" She was not only pleased, she was surprised.

"My mother used to make them into a salsa to use on fish tacos. And papaya cake. That was the best."

"I'll bet it was," she said, taking a sip and letting it glide down her throat. "What else can you cook?"

He smiled. "Well, those fish tacos I just mentioned. Although I try to eat on the healthy side. Tacos, enchiladas, tamales, burritos… they might be food for the gods, but when you work out every day the way I used to do they're also food for the waistline, and it's never been my desire to see mine grow." He patted his belly. "So far, so good. Oh, and I baked muffins, if you're interested. Healthy ones. No sugar, no butter."

"Then you really *are* a cook."

"Let's just say that I'm pretty sure I know my way around a kitchen. Not sure about anything gourmet, but the muffins were easy enough and the coffee was self-defense. One of the nurses in Afghanistan made coffee and it was horrible. I'd been there three days when I decided to take it over myself. Either that or no coffee, because it was eating away my stomach lining."

Lizzie laughed. "Was she that bad or were you just that gullible?"

Chuckling, he shook his head. "I may have known the answer to that at one time. But, since I don't now, I'd like to say she was bad and leave it at that."

Did he know how much he'd just revealed to her? It had come so easily now, after she'd spent so much time asking him questions he wouldn't or couldn't answer. Then suddenly… *this*. She wasn't going to get too excited, but she did hope it was a step forward. Hoped in a non-medical way, of course.

"So, what's on your agenda for today?' she asked, fully expecting him to draw a blank on that.

But the bright look coming over his face told her otherwise.

"Clothes. What I have on…that's it. Hand-me-downs left behind at the hospital. And shoes."

"Then we go shopping," she said, smiling.

He chuckled. "I think I'm one of those men who hates shopping."

"Amnesia doesn't cut it with me, Mateo. You need clothes—we get you clothes. And I love to shop, so prepare yourself. I could turn this into an all-day outing."

Mateo moaned. "My mother loves shopping and when I was young, I was forced to walk behind her, carrying her handbag. It was humiliating, especially to a little boy who was bullied and called a mama's boy, but it worked out because I worked out and got strong, which scared away the bullies." He smiled. "I wasn't really a fighter, but nobody ever knew that."

"Well, I won't ask you to carry my handbag unless you really want to."

Mateo moaned again. "Can't we just do it online?"

"What? And miss the fun of it?" Lizzie took another sip of the coffee and arched her eyebrows in surprise. "This is really good. I'm glad you remembered, because you can make it every morning you're here."

"Actually, I didn't remember the coffee. I remembered my mom and her love of everything papaya. This was just a lucky guess."

"So, Dr. Mateo Sanchez, skilled general surgeon…"

"*Former* general surgeon."

"I'll get on to that later. Maybe ask Janis to sit down hard on Dr. Jenkins and come up with a better treatment plan for you. Anyway, surgeon, chef, devoted son…what else?

"Not much technology sense."

"With the technology sense of a *nene*."

"What's a *nene*?" he asked.

"A goose."

She didn't know if a few memories really were slipping back or if these were things he'd simply kept to himself. Maybe to maintain some control? But she wasn't a shrink and, whatever the case was, she wouldn't ask.

"The official Hawaiian bird, actually."

"Seriously, with all the pretty little colorful birds everywhere, Hawaii chose a goose?"

She turned and strolled out to the lanai, where one of those "colorful birds"—a beautiful yellow-green *amakihi*—was sipping nectar from one of the nectar stations her dad had built. He'd had such a way with the birds, and with flowers. It was all still there—the colors, the care he'd taken… It was the first thing she went to look at every single morning of her life.

"The goose is a worthy bird," she said, stepping away from where the *amakihi* was feeding, so as not to disturb it. "They've been here half a million years, and they don't damage their habitat, so they've earned their place." She studied the muffin he was holding out for her. "I'm assuming papaya?"

"I was taught to take advantage of what you're given and be grateful for it."

"As long as you didn't climb the tree to get it, I'm good. But if you did…"

Mateo chuckled. "It was on the ground. Trust me. I may not remember a lot of things, but I do remember that head injuries and climbing up papaya trees don't mix. So, about my clothes…"

The headache wasn't bad, but it was too early to feel this tired. All he wanted to do was sit out on the lanai and doze, even though he'd been the one to suggest clothes-shopping. Too much, too soon. Making the coffee hadn't been bad, but baking the muffins had done him in.

He had to show her he was better, because if he didn't she'd pack him off to a hospital somewhere. There was nothing in him that wanted to go. In fact, even though he'd worked in a hospital, being turned into a hospital patient filled him with a fear that, when he thought about it, nearly paralyzed him.

He wanted to know why, but the answer didn't come to him when he tried to find that piece of himself. In fact, the more he visualized himself as a patient, the more he sweated and came close to an anxiety attack.

There were so many mysteries to his life still locked away that when he let it happen the frustration of it all led to a bad temper. But bad temper didn't solve his problems. So why go there? Why not detour around that roadblock? Because perhaps, at the end of the road, something better might be waiting for him.

It made sense. Now all he had to do was convince his logical mind to follow through. And that was the tough part. Because the other part of his mind still wanted to kick and rebel.

But not so much since Lizzie.

\* \* \*

"It's not too far. If you're up for a walk, it's about a mile."

She was dressed in a Hawaiian wrap-skirt, midi-length, yellow with a white floral print. Her shirt was a strappy white tank top that left a bit of her belly exposed. No bra. Hair tucked into a floppy straw hat with a few wild tendrils escaping, oversize sunglasses, and sandals.

Normally when she wasn't on duty she slouched around in terry shorts and an oversize T-shirt—*with* a bra. Going out with Mateo, for some uncharted reason, she wanted to look better. Funny how looking better made her feel better. Today she was feeling great. Something that hadn't happened very much recently.

"In fact, there are several shops, so you'll have a choice of clothing."

He stood, gave her an appreciative stare, and slipped into his sandals. "So what kind of clothing are we talking about?" he asked, as his gaze stopped on her exposed belly.

"Whatever you like. Do you remember the way you used to dress?"

She did like the three-day stubble on him,

and hoped it wouldn't go once he'd fixed himself up.

"I remember scrubs. A couple of suits… Don't know if I used to hate them then, but the thought of wearing a suit now…" He faked a gigantic cringe. "Pretty sure I slept in the buff."

"Too much information," Lizzie said, fighting back a grin—and a vision of Mateo in the buff.

As a doctor, she'd seen a lot of him, but not all. As a woman, her fantasies went well beyond—and that was dangerous.

*Mateo and her on the beach. On a blanket. Him rubbing sunscreen on her back, her shoulders, her thighs…*

Definitely dangerous territory, since she hadn't sorted out what kind of man, if any, she wanted in her future. "You've been in the Army for a while. You weren't sleeping in the buff there."

He laughed. "Well, maybe if I didn't in the past, it's something I might start doing in the future."

"Beach shorts. Tropical print, lightweight, somewhat baggy, stopping just at the tops of your knees. And a sleeveless T-shirt. Maybe some cargo shorts and a few cotton floral print button-up shirts. Also a pair of long khaki pants, with a white, breezy cotton shirt."

"And here I was, picturing myself more as a surf bum."

"Do you surf?" she asked, her mind still stuck on beach shorts and sleeveless T-shirts.

"Don't have a clue. Do you want to teach me?"

"Your last doctor advised you to stay away from activities like that for at least four months. It hasn't been four months."

"Then it's a good thing my last doctor no longer has a say, and my new friend just might be willing to show me some basic, non-threatening surfing moves. *If* she surfs."

"She does—and she's very good at it." She hadn't done nearly as much of it as she would have liked, owing to her dad's condition, alongside her hyper zest for work. But the thought of surfing with Mateo—well, at least bodyboarding—caused a little flush of excitement. "And if she decides to take you out, she's in complete control."

"I never thought she wouldn't be." He smiled.

"Anyway, my look is your decision. Except red. I won't wear red."

"Why not? With your dark skin color..."

He shook his head. "Too much like blood. I've seen more of that than I care to. Worn too much of that on me. No red."

"Red's overdone," she said, hiking her oversize canvas bag up to her shoulder. "But blue... *that's* a color."

"So is yellow," he said, smiling. "On you."

"Then you're the type of guy who notices these things about a woman, because in my experience—"

"What experience?" he interrupted.

"Well, in my case not much lately."

Not for years, to be honest. But Mateo didn't need to be burdened with her problems when he had enough of his own to wrestle with.

"You know what they say about all work and no play?" he quipped lightly.

"You're right about that," she returned.

"No, seriously. What *is* it they say?" His eyebrows knit into a frown.

"You don't remember?" she asked, highly suspicious of the twinkle in his eyes.

Was this the real Mateo coming out, or one

he was inventing just for her? She'd seen that in patients before—turning into the person they believed she wanted to see. The patient with excruciating headaches who refused to admit to them just to maintain a certain image. The patient with Parkinson's disease who denied his symptoms as a way of denying the disease.

People showed what they wanted—either to deny to themselves or put on a brave front for someone else—and she couldn't help but wonder if that was what Mateo was doing... showing her a side of himself he believed she wanted or needed to see. Maybe to maintain the roof over his head for a while? Maybe because he wanted to impress her?

Whatever was going on, she liked that spark, and hoped it was genuine.

He chuckled. "Of course I do. I was just wondering if you did, since you practically admitted you don't play. But you're not dull, Lizzie. Maybe not bursting with as much *joie de vivre* as you could be, or maybe should be, but definitely not dull."

"Well, dull is in the eye of the beholder, I

suppose. I've never thought of myself as particularly effervescent, though."

That was the truth. She was hard-working, serious, dedicated, and passionate about her career, but when it came to the personal aspects of her life, there'd never been much there. Not enough time. Or real interest.

"Then maybe you're not seeing what I'm seeing."

"Or maybe you don't know what you're seeing because you've forgotten what effervescence looks like in a person."

She motioned him to follow her off the lanai and then to the road in the front of the house. The hospital, and her home, were just a little way outside La'ie, on the north end of the island. It was out of the way, but bursting with life.

A lot of people at the hospital commuted up from Honolulu, or one of the larger cities to the south, like Kane'ohe, but she liked this area—liked the relative smallness of it, loved the people. Even though she'd left huge and disproportionate New York City for this, she couldn't imagine living anywhere else now.

Could she return to big city living? If she had

to. Would she want to, though? Not a chance. Living in paradise had spoiled her.

"So, what we're going to see will be surf shops for the most part. There are a couple of shops that specialize in other things—clothes that are more traditional, shoes, those sorts of things. And then there are the food vendors. All I can say is...*heaven*."

"Where every day is a holiday?"

"It can be, if that's what you want. Oh, and just so you know, I need to run into the hospital and sign some papers. You're welcome to come in with me, or wait outside if the old familiar surroundings make you uncomfortable."

"Snakes make me uncomfortable. And bullets. And I don't think I'm especially fond of clingy women, but I could be wrong about that one. Oh, and cats."

"You don't like cats?" she asked.

"Actually, I love cats. Love their independence and attitude. But I'm allergic."

"I've always wanted a cat. Or a dog. But we moved around too much, and my dad didn't think it would be practical, taking an animal with us. I had a goldfish once. His name was

Gus. Had to give him to a friend when we moved from Virginia to Germany."

"Because your dad was a surgeon. Career Army?"

"Yep—I was seeing the world at a very young age."

"And enjoying it?"

"Most of the time. Unless he had to leave me behind when he was in a combat zone. Even so, he gave me everything I needed and wanted."

Except a mother. Somewhere along the way her dad had decided he didn't have enough time or energy for another marriage, and Lizzie had often wondered if, in the end, having someone with him besides her might have helped him hang on to reality a little longer.

"It must have been tough on your dad, raising a daughter and maintaining his military career."

"It was what it was, and we managed," Lizzie said, as they walked along the narrow road, while people on bikes and scooters passed by on both sides of them. "When you never have a person in your life—like I didn't have my mother—you get used to it and make it work. My dad and I did."

"What happened to your mother?"

"She lost interest in the life we lived, then in my dad, and left us when I was about five. Died a couple years after that."

"So she never had a chance to make amends?"

"She could have. But she didn't want to."

"And your dad…?"

"He wasn't interested in trying before Alzheimer's hit. Then afterwards he didn't remember her at all."

"It couldn't have been easy on you, taking care of your dad the way you did."

"It wasn't—but I gave him the care he gave me when I was a child. I couldn't just…send him away somewhere."

"He isn't the reason you're here?"

"Actually, he is. They have an excellent treatment program at the hospital and I think it gave him more than anybody might have expected. But he lived at home because he loved it there, and I didn't have the heart to take that away from him. Especially his garden. When he was losing so many things in his life, his flowers still made him happy. It's nice, looking out every day, seeing a little bit of my dad still there. Somehow it makes the end seem easier. But don't get me wrong. I miss him. We had a tough life together, which was no one's fault, but he always tried. He just wasn't single father material, I suppose you could say. And... and now I look at his flowers and wonder if we both could have tried a little harder. Of course, Alzheimer's stepped in before we had much of a chance to do anything."

"How long has he been gone?"

As they walked down the path to the hospital Mateo took hold of her hand and she didn't pull away. It was nice feeling his touch. Having someone there who cared...at least for a little while. His hand was soft, and she could almost imagine it caressing her skin, giving her goosebumps.

Maybe she'd give *him* a few goosebumps as she ran her hand over his tight six-pack abs...

*Nice dream.*

"A year, now. One less brilliant surgeon in the world."

She noticed Mateo was starting to lag behind, so she slowed her pace to match his, but when she did he slowed down even more. This doctor clearly wasn't comfortable returning to the hospital, even if he was no longer a patient there.

"Do you need to take a break?" she asked, coming to a stop on the narrow road that led to the hospital's front door. It was lined with a rainbow of flowers and green, with draping wisps of vine hanging from the trees.

She'd always loved this path. It had welcomed her the day she'd first arrived, and every day since then. And this was part of her dilemma. To stay or to leave? Admittedly, she wasn't as restless as she'd been only a few weeks before, but her choice still wasn't clear. In other words, she didn't know what she wanted. She'd spent a lifetime living the life her dad had wanted for her, and now it was her turn to choose. But what?

Truly, she didn't know.

"No," Mateo said. "I'm fine. Just not excited to be back here." He took his place against a large lava rock, leaned casually back on it, and folded his arms across his chest. "You go do what you need to do, and I'll wait here."

He pointed to the little shop just down the

road. The front was totally open to the air, and several clothing racks spilled out onto the walkway.

"Or wander down there and pick out the most hideous clothes you can imagine."

"I'll be about ten minutes," she said, heading to the front door, walking along the path and crossing over the circular drive that led straight to the welcome sign: *Welina.* Greetings to you. It was a friendly place to some. But to some, not so much.

"I didn't know you'd be stopping by," Janis said, approaching the entrance to greet Lizzie.

"In the neighborhood." She glanced back over her shoulder to make sure Mateo was still there. "Looking for clothes for my…whatever he is."

"Speaking of which—how's he doing? We were worried until you called. But the thing that really concerns me is that he's living with you, Lizzie. That's not a good idea. Dependencies form. It may be difficult to get rid of him when the time comes."

"It was either that or the beach. And he was totally emphatic about not coming back here or going to the veterans' facility in California.

So…" She shrugged. "What was I supposed to do? He's not exactly ready to be out in the world on his own, yet."

She took another hasty glance and saw Mateo talking to a handful of strangers who were huddled around him. He did have that kind of personality—the kind that drew people in. He was making good use of that now.

"He's not supposed to be living with one of his doctors," Randy Jenkins said, approaching Lizzie and Janis.

"I'm not his doctor—never have been, never will be. And, not that it's any of your business, he's in the *ohana*, not in the house," Lizzie said, almost defensively.

"Do what you want," Randy said. "He's not a patient here, and right now he's on his own. So be his friend. I'm sure he needs that."

"Randy's right. It's your choice, Lizzie. But don't get too involved. I don't want to see you getting hurt."

"Hurt?"

"You know…feelings that aren't reciprocated. You're vulnerable right now, just like he is, and I don't want that playing against you."

"He's not like you think he is," she insisted.

"Or maybe he's not like *you* think he is," Janis countered. "Just be careful. That's all I'm saying. That, and put a leash on his desire to practice medicine. Because if people associate the two of you as medical partners and he makes a mistake, or forgets something..."

"What?" Lizzie spun around and, sure enough, Mateo was examining the wrist of a young boy who couldn't have been more than seven or eight. "Look, courier those papers over later and I'll sign them. Right now I think I've got to stop a doctor from practicing medicine."

"Easier said than done," Janis warned. "It's in his blood."

That was going to be a huge problem—teaching an old dog new tricks. Or completely rewiring the old dog until he was an entirely new one. Also, staying detached. That, perhaps, was going to be the hardest part, because Mateo was charming and she was not above being charmed, no matter how much she denied it to herself.

Why? Because she was lonely. Because he was attractive. Especially because he was attractive. Oh, and the charm that just oozed from his pores. She didn't know if that was really him, or a new Mateo he was trying on for size. But she liked it. Too much.

# CHAPTER FIVE

IT WASN'T LIKE he'd *meant* to practice medicine on a street corner, but he hadn't been able to help himself. The memory of the career that had been taken away from him kept poking at him, reminding him of who he'd used to be as opposed to who he was now. Nothing. That was who he was. Nothing. No one. A man without a memory living with a woman he barely knew.

"It's not broken," he told the little boy's mother. "Just sprained. It wouldn't hurt to go get an X-ray, but you could save yourself time and money by making a sling and keeping it immobile for a couple of weeks."

He was referring to a child who'd fallen and hurt his wrist. There was enough of the surgeon in him left that he could tell the difference between a sprain and a break. And while he shouldn't have been making the diagnosis, it had just happened. Child in pain, mother worried sick, him reaching out to help. It was not only the life he wanted, but the life he needed. If he wasn't a doctor, then who was he?

Someone from his own past, he decided as he rose to greet Lizzie—who, judging by the expression on her face, wasn't too happy with what he'd just done.

*Lizzie.*

He liked her.

She leaned a little too heavily toward the no-nonsense side, but he'd caught a few fleeting smiles and laughs, which only emphasized just how much she kept hidden.

"I suppose you're going to tell me I shouldn't be practicing medicine," he said, even before she'd reached him.

"You shouldn't. And without medical supplies?" she asked.

"With a hospital only a few feet away I assumed I was safe. And you know what they say: once a doctor, always a doctor."

"Well, don't tempt Fate, Mateo. You're standing on hospital property and you're lucky Janis is feeling tolerant. Just watch where you're dispensing bandages. OK?"

"Much ado about nothing," he said, grinning

at her as he purposely moved to the middle of the street.

"Why did you join the military?" she asked as they headed down the road to a little shop with a rack of brightly floral shirts on display. Typical casual wear that never failed to draw the tourists.

"Honestly? I don't know. Something drew me. Just don't know what it was." Mateo sighed as they stopped to look through the floral shirts. "Like so many other things. It's trapped in my mind. I can almost feel it there. But it won't surface."

"Give it time," Lizzie said, pulling out a blue floral print, then holding it up for Mateo.

"Well, time is something I certainly have a lot of, isn't it?" He shook his head at the print and she put it back. "I think my tastes run more toward T-shirts. At least I can't picture myself in something like that."

"How about you try it on, then decide?" Lizzie suggested, pulling down another one. This time it was a seafoam-green with white hibiscus flowers.

This wasn't working. Whatever the cause, he was getting anxious. Too many colors, too much stimulation. Too many people watching. At least it felt like they were. All eyes on him. Wounds. Blood. Expectations. So many of them. And he was supposed to save them all. But he couldn't. And they kept coming and coming...

"Mateo?" Lizzie said, giving his arm a gentle shake. "Where did you go?"

He blinked hard, then looked at her, not quite sure at first what was going on. Then it came back to him. It was simply another one of those bad recalls. They happened when he was awake. The nightmares came when he slept.

"To a place I'd rather not visit again."

He was wiped out. No activity for so long and now even the little things bothered him. Maybe it was emotional fatigue? Whatever the case, he wanted to be left alone. Wanted time to himself to think, to see if he could bring anything back. To forget there were so many things he no longer remembered.

"Do you mind if I go take a walk on the beach?"

"Are you OK going by yourself?" she asked.

"I'm perfectly capable of taking a walk by myself," he snapped, then instantly regretted it. "Look, things build up in me. Sometimes it feels like I'm a tea kettle just ready to go off. I didn't mean to…"

She laid a comforting hand on his arm and it sent chills all the way up and down his spine. "Pressure relief," she said. "It's common."

"How do you do it, Lizzie? How do you work with people like me, day in and day out, and not get burned out? Because from what I'm seeing there may never be a satisfying result in my future. Multiply that by all the patients you've cared for who are just like me, or worse… I'm surprised you don't have your own pressure relief to deal with."

"I do, actually."

She took hold of his arm and they headed off down the road toward the beach, strolling casually, like longtime lovers who knew each other's moves intimately.

"Some doctors find it in tobacco, drugs or alcohol. But I'm a little more passive. I like to watch the sunset. Or swim. And if I'm really angsty… I surf. I grew up—well…pretty much alone. Had to learn at a very young age to take care of myself. Because if I didn't, no one else would. Don't get me wrong. My dad did his best. It's just that so much of the time there wasn't enough left of him to *be* my dad. So my pressure relief? A lot depends on where I am. We lived in a snowy part of Germany for a while and I learned to ski. We spent time in Texas and I learned to ride a horse with the best of them. On Okinawa I learned to cook seafood. It all worked out."

They stopped just short of the beach, where she let go of him.

"And medical school?" he asked.

"It seemed like a good choice. And I was ready to get out on my own. See a different world than the one he gave me…do something different than what I'd always done, which was to make the best of any situation I landed in."

"Had to be tough."

"Not all the time. I like working at Makala-pua Pointe Hospital."

"But you don't love it?"

"To be honest, I'm not sure what I love. Most days it's my work, but some days it's just being lazy on the beach."

"Am I hearing mixed emotions?"

"Not mixed so much as changing. I love

being a doctor. That's the easy part. But the rest of it… Well, that's to be determined later."

"It happens a lot. It's called career burnout."

"I'm just tired right now. Once I've been away a little while I'll be anxious to go back."

"What if you're not?' he asked.

"Then I'll figure it out when the time comes. My dad burned out before his Alzheimer's. Just decided one day he was done. He'd already served a full career in the Army and he was in general surgical practice. It bothered him for a while, but he was happy in his new life. I'm tired, but not burnt out the way he was."

"And my being here isn't helping you rest, is it?"

"Actually, it's nice having someone around. I'm glad you're staying with me for a while. It makes my day…interesting."

Mateo chuckled. "I've been told I've done a lot of things, but making someone's day interesting…can't say I've ever heard that one. But seriously, Lizzie. If I get in the way tell me to go, and I will."

She stepped away from Mateo. "I'll see you later," she said, reaching out, giving his hand a squeeze. "Unless you decide to go somewhere else."

"Why would you say that?" he asked, wondering if she really wanted to get rid of him and if her hospitality had been offered on little more than a frayed thread.

Maybe he should go. Find a little place to call his own. Open a surf shop. Forget that he'd ever been a surgeon and content himself with whatever life brought his way.

Except…that wasn't him. He wasn't sure exactly who he was. But he was sure who he *wasn't*.

"Do you want me to leave, Lizzie? Be honest with me. Should I go?"

Lizzie shook her head. "When I invited you I meant it. Besides, where would you go?"

"That's a question for the ages, isn't it?"

He had enough money to get him through for a while. Or he could strike out on his own and hope that something good came of it. But truth be told the appeal of being alone was overrated—much the way Lizzie had claimed. And facing the world with only part of you intact was a scary proposition. He wasn't ready to try that. Not just yet.

*"One day at a time,"* his mother used to tell him, because that was the way they'd been forced to live. If she'd had dreams beyond that he'd never known what they were.

Did he have dreams beyond his stint in the military? Surely he must have. Or maybe he was like his mother—one day at a time. And now one day at a time with Lizzie.

He liked that. Probably more than he should and more than he had a right to. For now, though, it offered him something he no longer had—an identity. From that he would grow.

But in what direction?

It wasn't like she didn't trust him to find his way back. That part of Mateo was perfectly fine, and if he wanted to return here he would. Simple as that. She was distracted, though. And worried. It had been several hours and there was still no sign of him. Naturally that had made her think of her dad—that day he'd wandered away and hadn't been found.

That was the nightmare that still caused her to wake up sweating and shaking, thinking of him out there alone, sitting in the underbrush near Kapu Falls, waiting for death to take him.

Maybe it had been his choice—maybe that had simply been the way it ended for him. And now she was worried about Mateo. Probably needlessly. But all the same she couldn't settle until he was back.

"It's a nice offer," she said now to Kahawai, one of the wealthy property owners in the area.

He was a proper old man, with polished manners and a politeness that far exceeded anything she'd ever seen in another person. He'd come over to her house and brought cake. It was the way of the people here when one of their own was in trouble, and somehow he'd found out about Mateo. So they were eating cake and discussing business to keep her distracted—which wasn't working. Also, Kahawai had been trying to make her a serious offer for weeks.

"But I like where I am, and doing what I'm doing."

Even to her own ears her words didn't sound convincing.

Kahawai was offering to set up a small medical clinic for her to run. Something the immediate area lacked.

"It would be a good opportunity," he said,

slicing her a second, huge piece of cake. "For the community and for you."

They were sipping banana coladas on her lanai—non-alcoholic drinks made from bananas, pineapples, and a splash of Hawaiian fruit syrup. She'd done this with her dad in the beginning, until being sedentary had made him nervous. Then they'd strolled the beach, gone wading, or picked up seashells.

"But I've never practiced general medicine in a small clinic," she said. "I've always had a hospital and hospital resources to fall back on."

That was her excuse for turning down his offer, her reason for not moving on. And, while this was something she and her dad had talked about doing someday, the thought of doing it on her own was daunting. She wasn't sure she trusted herself enough. Not now, anyway.

"Well, I'd never been a property owner," said Kahawai. "But look at what I have now. Good fortune and my uncle's wealth smiled on me."

Lizzie glanced down the beach to see if she could spot Mateo, but it was practically deserted, as it always was at this time of the day. The locals had all gone home, and tourists tended not to know about this spot. That and the fact that it was all privately owned, which meant no trespassing.

"He'll be back in his own time," Kahawai said. "Maybe he wanders the beach like you do, night after night, trying to find yourself. This doctor with no memory…does he mean something to you?"

"He has a memory," she defended, almost too quickly. "He just doesn't have… Let's just say that he's suffered some trauma and now he's trying to come to terms with it."

"And he's living with you until he's cured?"

"He's staying in my *ohana* until he knows what he wants to do. Big difference."

Kahawai grinned as he stood, preparing to leave. "Well, whatever the case. My offer stands. And if your roommate would like to work with you I'll have a place for him as well. I understand he was a great surgeon in his day."

"Good news travels fast around here, doesn't it?" Lizzie said, trying not to give in to the anxiousness awakening in her.

"We're like family, Lizzie. When you decide you want to be part of that family there'll be a place for you."

He carried his glass into the kitchen and exited through the front door, leaving Lizzie alone on the lanai, watching for Mateo.

What if he had decided to move on? Had he taken his things? What few things he had?

Suddenly the impulse hit her to head off to the beach and look for him. But, racing past the *ohana*, she found him standing on the door-step, simply watching the night drop down on the beach.

"Looks like you're in a hurry to get some-where," he commented, moving over to allow her room enough to stand there with him.

She squeezed in next to him, determined not to tell him what she was up to. She was his landlord, not his keeper, and she had to keep reminding herself of that.

"Just out for a walk," she said, enjoying the feel of being pressed next to him.

"A walk with a vengeance. You looked like a lady with a purpose." He slid his arm around her waist, and she readjusted to allow it.

"Just in a hurry."

"You and nobody else. That's what I've been observing—the way people take things at their own pace. They don't seem so caught up in modern life here."

"That's all I'm *ever* caught up in," she said.

"Did you learn that from your dad?"

"Maybe. I was always trying to keep up with him."

"Did you ever succeed…before his illness?"

Lizzie shook her head. "He was a tough man. When he had time for me, if I didn't take it he'd move on in the blink of an eye."

"And that's how you want to be? Like your dad?"

Lizzie laughed. "To be honest, I want to be just the opposite of what he was. I want to have a life *around* my work. He wanted nothing *but* work. Sometimes, if I catch myself doing or saying something he might have, I pull back… do just the opposite."

"And that's your problem now. You want to walk totally away from him and you don't know how."

"You should have been a shrink, Mateo." She leaned her head against his shoulder. "You have…depth."

"That surprises you?"

"Well, you haven't exactly been forthcoming about who you really are, have you?"

"It's easier to stay safe that way. I learned that when I was young, trying to make it through school with good grades rather than a bad reputation. Then again in medical school, where brown skin wasn't exactly the norm."

"Did that bother you much?" she asked.

"When I was young, yes. But most kids suffer at the hands of other kids one way or another. When I started discovering who I was…" He chuckled. "Well, let's just say that I know who I am, but in totally different terms now."

"It's almost funny how a man with amnesia may know more about himself than I know about myself."

She should leave now. Get away from him while she could. Because as intimacy wove around them she was becoming fully aware that Mateo was the man who might make a difference in her life—if she allowed it. But her legs were too weak to support her body and too shaky to move her away from there. And the humid night, even with the cool spritz coming from the air-conditioning in the *ohana*, surrounded her, held her in place…which allowed his kiss in.

Just like the way Lizzie felt, Mateo's kiss was unsteady at first. Tentative, with a masterful edge just waiting to break through. But he held back. Allowed time to pull her into his arms, tight enough so he could smell the faint scent of gardenias in her hair but loose enough to let her respond to his touch. Her arm, caressed by his, burned, and yet she shivered.

"Are you cold?" he asked, his breath warm on her neck.

Lizzie instinctively tilted her head to look up at him. He was tall, much taller than her, and his shoulders were broad…something she'd tried hard not to observe at the hospital in anything other than a professional way. But now her profession didn't stand between them, and she admired what she saw the way any woman would admire a beautiful man.

"Just…unaccustomed…" she replied, her voice barely above a whisper.

She thought briefly about the colors of the evening sky—the golds and oranges, all the colors that took on a different meaning tonight, other than simply being the colors of another night alone on the beach. Stars by the thousands were twinkling. And she was gazing out on the empty sea, her empty life, her empty world.

All full now—if only for a moment.

Mateo shifted just enough to catch her off-balance and push her against the door frame. In a heartbeat he grabbed her and held her tighter, his dark eyes staring intently into hers. Just a breath between them with no place to hide.

"To what?" he asked. "What are you unaccustomed to?"

"You…me…us. All of this. I've held myself back from it."

"Why?"

"Because there was nothing I wanted to become accustomed to. Nothing…no one who mattered. And being like that has become a habit. I'm always too tied up with…other things."

"Maybe this will break your habit," he said.

His voice was deep and intense. So much so, his meaning was clear. And when their lips met his hold on her tightened even more.

He was pulling her into him, pressing himself into her.

It wasn't like she wanted to be somewhere else. She didn't. This moment—right here, right now—that was all there was. *Her* moment. And as her eager mouth fused to his she forgot who they were, where they were, or why they were. None of that mattered now. Nothing mattered but the tip of his tongue brushing her lips and the way she welcomed the urgent thrusting that sent even more shivers racing through her body.

Mateo had expected some heat just from being so close to her. Something mildly pleasant from almost touching. Then actually touching. But the sizzle, the pure magnetic draw of her—that was what caught him off guard. And not just the way she responded to him, but the way he responded to her. Like he'd never kissed a woman before.

The moment his lips touched hers, ever so briefly, and he cupped her neck with his hand, she arched backward, allowing him more of her. And as his thumb caressed the silken flesh of her throat, and she quivered hard against him, he pulled her even tighter to him, to close the gap, to feel the contours of her.

Damn, but her lips were soft. Too soft. And he fought to call back every bit of reason that was escaping him.

But before reason took over, he pressed his lips hard to hers, and felt the twining of her leg with his calf. A tiny, pleading sound was liberated from her throat—and that was when he lost his control. His cool. His will to keep this impersonal. That was when Mateo bent his head and seized that sound, drawing it between his lips and holding it there, for fear that once he backed away it would be gone, and they would return to normal.

His emotions were too close to the surface now. Too naked. Too close to revealing parts of him he didn't even know in himself. Which scared him.

So rather than thinking about it, rather than letting his pure, raw emotions take over, he kissed her with everything inside him—fear for the future, desire for someone he didn't know, desperation for what would become of him once Lizzie was out of his life.

Because she *would* be out of his life. There

may have been mere millimeters between them now, but those millimeters would soon turn into worlds. And those different worlds would separate them.

The thought of that pulled him back.

"Well, that's one thing you certainly haven't forgotten," Lizzie said, brushing her fingers across her red swollen lips.

"It's a natural response to you, Lizzie. Surely you've seen it building?"

"Sometimes I miss the obvious. Partly because I want to and partly because I don't put myself out there."

"How is it with me?"

She raised her fingertips to her lips. "Nice. Very, very nice."

He'd almost hoped she would say something like they couldn't do it again, or it had been terrible. But the smile on her face told him otherwise. Which wasn't good because already he wanted more, when there was no more to give. Or to have.

He was sitting on the lanai, sipping a fruit juice, watching the darkness surround him. It was a good place for him to be, because she was too confused to make much sense of their situation. In fact, broiling a *mahi-mahi*, a simple task, was proving to be almost more than she could handle right now.

"So, reason it out," she said aloud as she chopped the mangoes, cilantro, green onions, and bell peppers to top the fish. "He kissed you, or you kissed him. Either way, it was a kiss."

Perhaps the only kiss she'd ever had that was worth remembering.

"He enjoyed it…you enjoyed it."

Truer words never spoken. But was there anything beyond what they had already? She didn't know, and she was pretty sure he didn't either.

Lizzie drew in a heavy sigh. Her last relationship, which had been her marriage to Brad, was a disaster of epic proportions, and even though it was so far in the past, she wasn't sure she was ready for something else. She'd been played—expecting everything, getting nothing. Maybe she'd even let herself be played, believing what she wanted to believe, seeing what she wanted to see.

Because in the end their collapse had come

as no real surprise to her. There'd been hints. His self-imposed curfew. The texts he'd sent when he'd thought she wouldn't notice. Other women. Another life.

"Mateo isn't married," she argued with herself.

But even if she were to get involved, the one thing that frightened her was his lack of memory. Would she always have to be on guard for him, like she'd been for her dad? Always nervous when he was late getting home? Or when she couldn't find him in the house?

She'd lived that life once and honestly didn't know if she had it in her to do it again. The circumstances might be different, but she saw so much sameness. Or maybe that was what she wanted to see. Something to keep her at a safe distance, because she honestly didn't know where she was going.

What would happen if he found himself again and he wasn't the man she thought he was? She'd certainly been in the dark about her husband, and perhaps that was what scared her most. She was falling for this Mateo, but there might be another one waiting to emerge. Having fallen in love with one man who'd turned out to be someone else…she wasn't going near that again.

"And the moral of that story," she said to her salsa, "is don't get involved."

She glanced out the sliding glass door, only to catch herself wondering how much that kiss had changed things. Or if it had changed things between them at all. They were, quite simply, house-owner and houseguest. End of story. At least, she hoped so.

"Doc Lizzie!" someone yelled into her kitchen window. "Come quick. I think he's dead."

That snapped Lizzie from her doldrums and she grabbed her medical bag, clicked on her outside floodlights, and ran out the lanai door to follow the college-age man down to the beach, where one of his buddies, who'd had a little too much to drink, was lying unconscious in the sand.

Immediately she dropped to her knees on the left side of him, and saw Mateo drop to his knees on the right and lay his fingers on the man's neck to check for a pulse. He tried a couple different places as Lizzie inflated the blood pressure cuff, then shook his head grimly.

"Nothing," he said, taking hold of the man's wrist to check for a pulse there.

When Lizzie looked over at him for an answer, he shook his head again.

"I can't get a blood pressure on him, either." She looked up at the young man's buddy. "What happened?"

"We were surfing. Real good tides at night around here. And he fell off his board. Don't know what happened after that. Maybe it hit him…"

"Is he drunk?" Mateo asked.

"We've had a few beers. Nothing serious."

"That's what they all say," Lizzie said to Mateo. "A few beers and a surfboard can get you dead." She said that for the benefit of the young man's buddy. "What's his name?"

"Teddy. Teddy Chandler."

"Teddy, can you hear me?" Mateo yelled, giving the young man a hard thumb in the middle of his chest.

A sternum-rub, as it was called, was a technique used for assessing the consciousness level of a person who wasn't responding to normal interactions such as voice commands. In Teddy's case there was no reaction.

"Call for an ambulance," Mateo shouted, while Lizzie put her ear almost all the way down on Teddy's mouth to see if there was any discernible breathing.

When she could find nothing, she checked for a pulse again. Like before, it wasn't there. So she commenced CPR, placing the heel of one hand on the center of Teddy's chest at the nipple line.

As she positioned herself to start the compressions, Mateo took an IV set-up from her medical bag and inserted it into Teddy's vein—right arm, just below the bend. He attached a saline bag to it, but nothing else.

"Epinephrine could cause severe brain damage," he said, more to himself than Lizzie.

"You remembered that?"

"I remember some of the newer studies stating epi is contraindicated in cardiac arrest."

Lizzie stopped her chest compressions long enough to assess Teddy for breath sounds, but still he wasn't breathing.

Mateo opened Teddy's airway by tilting his head back and lifting his chin. Then he pinched the man's nose closed, took a normal breath, and covered his victim's mouth with his own, giving him two one-second breaths, hoping to see the natural rise and fall of his chest.

Still nothing was happening.

He gave two more breaths, followed by Lizzie, who administered thirty chest compressions. Then they repeated it all.

The second set of compressions caused Teddy to vomit and spit out seawater, and then he sputtered to life, blinking hard, and reeking of far more than a few beers.

"Can I go home now?" the young man muttered, trying to sit up even as Mateo forced him back onto the sand.

"The only place you're going is to the hospital," Lizzie told him. "In a saltwater near-drowning water is pulled out of the bloodstream, and then it pools in the lungs, where it's thicker than normal blood, and can cause heart damage since your heart isn't used to pumping hard enough to circulate the thickened blood."

"In other words," Mateo chimed in, "you may have messed up your heart, so you need to have it checked out."

"Will it hurt?" Teddy asked.

Mateo looked across at Lizzie and smiled. "Probably. But that's what happens when you drink too much and then think you can conquer the surf. It doesn't happen that way, Teddy. Worldwide, one person drowns every two minutes, and while half of those are children, the half that *aren't* children are largely made up of men who take risks. Drinking and surfing is a risk—you got lucky that your buddy knew where to go to fetch a doctor. Normally it doesn't turn out that well."

Lizzie stood and brushed sand from her knees. Mateo was impressive. Besides that, he was a very good doctor, and for the first time she wondered if there might still be a place in medicine for him. What he'd done and what he'd remembered… Heroic didn't even begin to describe it.

Surely there was a place for him?

Someplace better than where he was now?

Someplace where she wouldn't be so tempted by him?

And, make no mistake. Mateo tempted her in ways no man ever had before.

\* \* \*

*"It's you they need out there, Doc. Not some other medic. This is Freddy. You've got to go. Got to go... Got to go..."*

*The soldier faded from view then reappeared in an ambulance, motioning for Mateo.*

*"Hurry up. Hurry up."*

*"But I need to be here," Mateo protested. "Incoming."*

*"Go," his nurse was telling him.*

*She was pointing at the door where, just outside, the ambulance awaited.*

*"Go, Doctor. It's your duty. This is Freddy."*

*But the faces in the hall were blurring together. And the soldiers with those blurred faces were all pointing at the door.*

*"Go!" they were screaming as he dropped to his knees, shut his eyes, and held his hands over his ears. "Go, Mateo!"*

*He opened his eyes and he was alone. Just him in the makeshift hospital. And the ambulance. No one to drive him. But the voices— they were still in his head.*

*"Go!" Mateo screamed, then bolted up in bed, sweaty and shaken.*

*He knew he had to go, but he didn't know where.*

*Dear God, he didn't know where.*

Lizzie could hear him scream through her open window. This was his battle to win, not hers. But she desperately wanted to help him through it. Except she couldn't. These nightmares he was having were taking him on a journey he had to walk alone. The answers he needed were there. But they were his to find, not hers to reveal.

She believed that now, as much as she ever had. Still, as she went to her own bed she was shaken. And silent tears slid down her cheeks. She wanted to fight his battles, do away with his demons. But in the end that would only make her feel useful—it would do nothing to help Mateo.

As she laid her head on her pillow and shut her eyes all she could see was an image of someone drowning. Mateo. He was walking into the water and she was the only one there to pull him out. But she couldn't.

That was her nightmare for the rest of the night. He was drowning and she couldn't get to him, the same way she hadn't been able to get to her dad when he was dying. She was letting them down, letting them both down. And she didn't know how to fix it.

# CHAPTER SIX

"You OK?" Mateo asked.

He was concerned about Lizzie. She hadn't said a word in over an hour. Sitting there in the sand, staring at the water, she seemed almost like a statue. A beautiful statue, maybe of a goddess watching over the sea.

"I cleaned up the mess from last night's burnt mahi-mahi and salvaged the salsa to put over something else. But I'm not sure what, since you don't keep a lot of groceries in your pantry."

"Because I rarely eat at home. When Dad was in better shape he loved to cook, but then when I took over we ate very simply. If I couldn't fix it in under thirty minutes, we went out. At least until he couldn't do that anymore. Then, with everything he needed from me in the evenings, I usually just brought something home."

"Did you have someone helping you?"

"I had a couple different people who were available when I wasn't here. One was a student nurse, the other a retired physical therapist. They were good with Dad, but he always wanted me, and sometimes he'd get so belligerent I'd have to leave work to come take care of him." She shook her head. "My father was a lieutenant colonel in the Army, and toward the end he didn't even know his own name."

"I didn't either," he said. "Not for several days. I can't imagine how it would be to lose yourself entirely. Even with just pieces of me gone, I get frustrated. And that's nothing compared to what your dad went through. I'm sorry for that, Lizzie. I suppose we tend to think we're invincible, but the scariest thing that happened to me was waking up in Germany when the last thing I remembered was performing a surgery in a desert outpost hospital. Nobody would tell me what was going on, and I certainly didn't have the capacity at that point to figure it out."

He sat down in the sand next to her, handed her a glass of fresh fruit juice, and took her hand.

"I felt so...alone. I imagine that's how your

dad felt when he knew he was losing his memory. It's not an easy thing to face."

She scooted closer and grasped his hand a little tighter. "He wasn't cooperative, either."

Mateo laughed. "Either? Which implies what?"

"You haven't been cooperative. So much so, you got kicked out. And now you're homeless. And, while I'm beginning to see what I believe is the real you, you're still not trying to get better. There's outpatient therapy and private counseling available. It's just a few steps from your door. And yet you've never ventured down there to see if there's anything for you. It's disappointing, Mateo. It's like you enjoy being a step out of time."

"Lucky you took me in, then, isn't it?"

"Is it? I mean, sometimes you act like this is a real relationship. That kiss, for instance. Was it the start of something? Was it meant to be manipulative? What *was* it, Mateo? I spilled my guts to you about how unsure I am and got nothing back. Why is that?"

"Did you ever consider that it might have simply been a kiss? That I'm attracted to you and it just happened?"

"See—that's the problem. You're happy taking the easy way out in the things you do, the things you say. When you walked away from your treatment program did you even stop to think what you were doing? I mean, no one wants to stay in hospital, but if you've got no place else to go—"

"When I was in Afghanistan a lot of widowed women with children came to the hospital," he said, remembering how they would show up out of desperation and hope someone there had a solution for them. "The best we could do was a meal, sometimes a blanket, and the few provisions we could scrounge. It was heartbreaking, seeing all those people with no place to go."

"But that's you," Lizzie said.

"That was me before that particular memory returned. If all these images had been coming back, I might have made a different choice. But I didn't, so here I am. What can I say? I made a mistake. Made several of them. And, at the risk of repeating them, it's easier just to keep myself…isolated."

"Because that's what you think you deserve?"

"I can't answer that because I don't *know* what I deserve or don't deserve."

"That's something best left up to you to figure out. It's a fine line, Mateo. You're doing so much better than anyone might have expected, but you've still got a long way to go. And I'm not going to be the one to tip you in any direction."

"I know. The rest of it's up to me. But I haven't quit, Lizzie. I just don't respond well to pushing."

"Because you've always been in charge and suddenly you're not?"

"That probably explains part of it. But the rest… I know it's not me. At least, I hope it's not." He shrugged. "I'm not very happy with myself, but I need to know why I do and say what I do before I can fix it."

"If you're not sure of the problem, how can you fix it?"

"Maybe I can't. I don't know. But the one thing I do know is that kiss…it was real. As real as any kiss I've ever had. And I meant to do it, Lizzie. You know, to seize the moment?"

"Am I just a moment?" she asked.

He shook his head. "You've never been just a

moment since the first time I set eyes on you. Want to know what I thought at the time?"

"I'm not sure."

Mateo chuckled. "I'll tell you anyway. You'd hurried up and down the hall several times that morning, always in a such a rush. But then one time you poked your head in my door and said, 'Hello.' Then you were gone. I thought you had the most kissable lips I'd ever seen. You were there maybe two seconds, but in those two seconds I knew you were somebody I wanted to know better. And kiss."

"Seriously? You wanted to kiss me?"

"I'll swear on a stack of hibiscus seeds that's what I wanted to do."

Lizzie reached up and brushed her fingers lightly over her lips. "I suppose I should be flattered."

"Not flattered. But hopefully in the mood for another one someday."

"Time will tell," she said, when she'd really intended to say no. But why limit her options? Especially since she *was* attracted to him? So, time *would* tell, wouldn't it?

Mateo put his arm around Lizzie's shoulder and the two of them stood at the water's edge, looking out on the ocean. It was nearly a perfect night. The skies were clear, the waters calm.

"When I was a kid, sometimes we'd go to Lake Chapala or even the Manzanillo coastline to swim. I was too young to realize we were too poor to stay in any of the nice hotels or eat in the nice restaurants the way most of the people were. To me, it was a treat just getting to go. So we'd pile in the car—my mother, my aunt, my grandmother, and her sister—take along packed food, and have the best day playing in the water. Then one time one of the kids from a hotel called me a *pobre niño*. Loosely translated that means poor kid. I didn't understand what he meant, or what he was implying, but I knew it wasn't good. After that we quit going and my mother never explained why. But I don't think she wanted me touched by that kind of ugliness. Then we moved to California and it was all forgotten. But the look of horror on her face that day... It broke my heart and I didn't even know why.

"Kids can be cruel," she said.

"Not just kids. It's in all of us, I think. But most people are aware of how their words can hurt and don't use them maliciously. On nights like this…perfect nights… I think back to how my little piece of perfection was ruined by a couple of words, and I wonder if the kid who used them against me even remembers."

"But they made you stronger, didn't they?"

"Only because I allowed them to. When you're five, though, all you see is something that's been taken away from you when it wasn't your fault."

"Which is why you became a doctor?"

"Actually, we lived in a small flat behind a doctor's office. He let me go in and read some of his books. Most of them I didn't understand, but by the time I was nine I knew that being a doctor was my calling. When he retired he gave me all those medical references, which were horribly outdated, but I loved reading them. I almost got myself kicked out of school for taking one or two of them to class rather than my textbooks. And you?"

"It was all I knew. I was talking serious medicine with my dad when I wasn't much more than a toddler, and by the time I was old enough to choose a career path medicine seemed like the logical choice. I knew it, I loved it, and most of all I knew what was involved. So there was never any doubt."

"Well, I went through the fireman, cowboy, and astronaut phases, but somehow I always tied them into medicine." He chuckled. "For a while I pictured myself making house calls on horseback."

"I have a friend—a nurse practitioner—who makes calls in the mountains in the east, where it's totally underdeveloped. She goes by horse because the roads are impassable."

"Well, then, bring on the cowboy hat and turn me loose."

Mateo looked out on the ocean again and watched a small child who was trying to swim toward the shore. She seemed to be alone, fighting the water, and his instinct kicked in.

Without a word, he suddenly dashed out, dived beneath the waves, and got to the child just as she was about to go under. Pulling her close to his chest, he held her for a moment until her cries quieted and the realization that she was safe set in, then he brought her back to shore, where several people had gathered, watching the rescue.

Lizzie spread out a blanket for the little girl,

but stepped back when Mateo laid her there and did a quick check to make sure she wasn't injured. By the time he was finished the beach patrol had pulled up with the girl's mother, who was crying as she dropped to her knees next to her daughter.

"She's fine," Mateo assured the woman, who'd bundled her daughter into her arms. "I'm a doctor and I did a quick check. She's more shaken than anything. But you're free to take her to the hospital..."

The woman wiped away her tears and looked at Mateo. "No, I believe you."

"What happened?" he asked gently.

"She wandered off. I think she loses track of where she is and just..." The woman batted back tears. "Susie is autistic. She's smart. But sometimes she doesn't pay attention. And if I turn my back..."

"I understand," he said, laying a reassuring hand on the woman's arm.

"Sometimes she just gets away from me. She's full of life and thinks she can do anything, but..." The woman scooped up her daughter and followed the beach patrol officer back to his car. Before she left, she turned back to Mateo. "So many people are critical when something like this happens. I appreciate your kindness, Doctor. More than you know."

Mateo stood there for a moment after they drove off, then turned to face Lizzie, who'd come up behind him and now stood there quietly, holding on to his arm.

"Just when you think your problem is the worst in the world, you run into someone who has something going on that's far worse. I used to see that in surgery. Back when I was a resident, sometimes I'd get a little depressed that I wasn't assigned to one of the bright, shiny new medical hospitals—and then I'd get this patient whose life was hanging by a thread. It always made me realize how lucky my lot in life really was."

"I didn't even see her, Mateo. We were looking at the very same thing and I didn't see her."

"I wasn't sure I did, either. It was a gut reaction."

Lizzie blew out a long sigh. "Well, whatever it was, I think I just saw a miracle happen."

He chuckled. "Not a miracle, Lizzie. That was me in my element. Me the way I was and the way I want to be again."

"Do you ever wonder what your life might have been like if you'd chosen to do something different?" she asked. "Like me. I had a music scholarship—I could be playing in some world-class symphony orchestra now. But here I am, and I'm not always happy about it."

"Because…?"

Lizzie shook her head. "I don't know. That's the thing. I always wanted to be like my dad, but in the end he wasn't the man I knew. Of course I wasn't the woman *I* knew by then, either."

"As far as I know I always wanted to do what I do…did. My mother worked hard to get me through school. She even gave up living near her family to relocate to another country, so I'd have a better chance at achieving my dream. But there was that summer I worked on a ranch in Arizona. I was twelve, maybe thirteen. My mother took a job feeding the ranch hands while the real cook was off on maternity leave. By the end of the summer I was convinced my destiny was to be a cowboy, not a doctor. But then, on my very last day, I fell off a horse, broke my arm, and went back to my original plan. I think my mother was glad of that, because she hadn't worked so hard only to see her son herding cattle and mending fences. Not that there's anything wrong with that. But it's not me. Of course, being a surgeon isn't me anymore, either."

"But there's a place for you, Mateo. I'm not sure where it is, or what it is, but skills like yours would be wasted mending fences. Maybe I can help? As a friend?"

"Well, if you find that place, let me know. I'm getting tired trying to figure it out. And so far the road just keeps getting longer and longer, with no guarantees at the end of it. I mean, what's the point of involving you, or anybody else, when nothing about my outcome can be predicted? What could you do to help me, Lizzie? Be specific. What can really be done to help me? Especially when I'm still in a place where when I wake up half the time I have to re-orient myself? What day is it? What time? Where am I?"

"What I can do is make sure you're not going wherever it is you're going alone. The choices must be yours, Mateo. But I can be the support you need."

"Why would you want to tie your life to mine

that way? You've already been through some-thing similar once. Why go back for more?"

To give herself another chance?

To go back and find an outcome that wasn't like her dad's?

She hadn't told him the full story yet, but he'd gathered enough to know that she blamed herself for his death. So was this Lizzie's need to find another path the way he was trying to do?

"Because I can," she said simply.

He tilted her chin up and stared into her eyes. So much beauty there, yet so much sadness. Would it even be fair of him, pulling her into his problems when what he could see told him she had enough of her own?

"My previous doctors didn't get me. They were excited when they discovered I still knew how to peel a banana, when what I really wanted to know was how to perform a carotid endarterectomy. You know, the big things—like how to clear the carotid artery of a block-age, how large an incision I should make in the sternocleidomastoid muscle. I know the result could be a stroke, depending on the percentage of blockage, but I can't run through the procedure in my mind without stumbling. What kind of scalpel did I prefer? Or clamp? What kind of impact would the procedure have on my patient's quality of life? It's all there..." He tapped his head. "But not in the way it's supposed to be—which makes me doubt so many other things in my life, including my decision to leave the veterans' facility and come here, only to be so uncooperative that I get kicked out. That's not me. I know that. And yet when I see what I do..."

He shook his head.

"And then to draw you into the middle of it just because you're willing to be there with me... So much of me wants that, Lizzie. But I don't have the right to take over your life that way. I know I'm a problem. I know I do exactly the opposite of what I need to be doing. And to put all that stress on your shoulders, just because I want you at my side..."

"We all hobble through life with one problem or another, Mateo. I think there's something here for you. Not me, per se. But something else. I'd like to be like you are—the one who spots the little girl in the water and saves her before anybody else even knows she's there.

And I can help you because what you're going through is impossible to face alone. I'm sure of that. And I do like you, in spite of yourself."

She expected a kiss, and maybe he did too, but instead he reached up, ran his thumb down the side of her cheek to her neck, and then placed the first of his kisses. Butterfly kisses that made her toes curl.

Everything inside her told her to back away, but she was fighting all that was feminine inside her that compelled her harder into his arms, revealing more of her neck to him. And as he took what she was offering her lips parted with a sharp intake of breath.

The sound of her shallow, rapid breathing as he kissed her caused her to desire more. And as if he'd read her mind, he cupped the back of her neck and kissed her deeply, gently, and so quietly she had to open her eyes to make sure he was still there.

He was, and the look in his eyes told Lizzie that he was desperate to explore. As desperate as she was. Which for the first time didn't scare her. Nothing about Mateo did. And that was the problem. The barriers keeping her away from this man had failed, and she wasn't sure she wanted to put them back in place.

No, that was wrong. She was sure she *didn't* want to put them back in place. And again, in another first, she didn't really care.

"You won't get anyplace close to where you want to be if you're alone."

"I've always been alone."

"Not really. You have a mother. I do understand why you don't want to burden her with this. But she knows things you want to know, and maybe reaching out would be good for both of you."

It was breakfast time again, and she was sitting on the beach, eating a bowl of fruit. She'd spent the night in her room; he'd stayed in the *ohana*. But whose choice had it been to remain circumspect? She wasn't sure, to be honest. Maybe it had been mutual. A natural pulling back of feelings for fear they were getting in too deep too quickly.

Well, it sounded good, anyway. But waking up alone hadn't felt so good. So maybe they were just about the moment and nothing else. All she knew was that she'd felt a cold, hard lump in her stomach when he'd walked her to her door and then, without so much as a kiss to the cheek, gone around to the *ohana*.

He shook his head. "I don't want people that close to me."

"Even me?" she asked.

"I don't know. When I'm with you, that's all I want. When I'm not, I'm cursing myself for being so stupid letting you in."

"You sure do know how to flatter a girl," she said, trying not to sound as grumpy as she felt.

"No offense intended."

"As I'm beginning to learn. But here's the thing, Mateo. There's an offer on the table from last night and the answer is simple. Yes or no? Do you want me standing with you? And this time, please don't dodge the question."

He searched her face for his answer, and all he saw was genuine honesty. This was a big step, though. He'd been wandering alone for a long time, and to invite somebody in scared and excited him at the same time. Because he didn't want to walk away from Lizzie. She made him feel…hopeful.

Swallowing hard, Mateo said, "Yes," in a voice that was barely more than a whisper.

"Then that's where I'll stand."

"Until you get too involved for your own good."

Lizzie bent over and brushed the sand off her legs. "That's for you to figure out, Mateo, if and when it happens. Anyway, I'm going down to The Shack to have some juice and forget everything else for a while. You're invited to join me, or you can stay here and eat whatever you care to fix. Your choice."

"Well, with such a gracious invitation on the table how could I refuse?"

He wasn't in the mood for crowds this early in the day. In fact, he'd hoped to spend some quiet time on the beach with Lizzie, listening to the far-off strains of the waves lapping the shore and watching a ship make its lazy way through one of the channels.

There was so much clutter in his head. So many things darting in and out. And he didn't know which were real and which were not.

Lizzie was real, though. As real as any woman he'd ever met. And their kiss the night before had been about the *realest* kiss he'd ever had. It could have led to more. Maybe it should have done.

But Lizzie was surrounded by barriers that were surrounded by their own barriers and more barriers after that. He couldn't see her letting them down—not for him, not for anyone. Couldn't see her ever giving in to the moment, even though she almost had during their kiss.

"The beach is no place to be alone on a beautiful morning like this, so maybe I'll tag along. Unless you choose to be alone," he said, hoping that wouldn't be the case.

"Does anyone ever really choose to be alone?" Lizzie asked. "Or is that a decision forced on them by circumstances?"

"Guess it depends on the person and what he or she really wants from life. Sometimes I'm in the mood to be solitary, sometimes I'm not."

"But given the choice between the two?"

"Can I choose to be flexible?"

Lizzie laughed. "You can choose anything you like, Mateo. It's your life."

"Not lately it hasn't been."

"Well, it's up to you to fix that, isn't it?"

"You really put a lot of faith in me to do the right thing, don't you?"

When they arrived at The Shack the place was busy, as always, so she chose to sit on a log under a banyan tree.

"You were a surgeon. I'm guessing a whole lot of people put their faith in you to do the right thing. You, too. You *did* put faith in yourself, didn't you?"

"I did. But it went with the job. I owed the people in my care the best I could give them."

"Plus all the military pressures on top of that. Sometimes I think that's what made my dad too old too soon. He never knew how to relax, even when he had time off."

"Do you relax very often?" Mateo asked. "Apart from your vacations, do you ever make time to do something for yourself? Something you enjoy?"

"I surf. Not as much as I'd like, like I said before, but I do get out there on my board once a week, or more, if I can fit it in. So, what do *you* do?"

"Long in the past I played guitar in a little band. I also painted… Nothing fine. Don't have that kind of skill. But I did murals on the sides of buildings. Urban art is what they call it now, and I really enjoyed it. I've always wondered if any of my work is still out there or if some other urban artist has come along and painted over it."

"You should go see," Lizzie said. "Maybe even create something new."

She flagged down the server, who was hustling his way through the growing crowd.

"I'll keep it simple," she told him. "Portuguese sausages and white rice, *lilikoi* juice and *malasadas*. They're like a fried doughnut," she explained to Mateo.

The server looked to Mateo for his order. "I'll have the same," he said, and then to Lizzie, "I'm trusting your judgment on this."

"Hope that extends to things other than breakfast," she said.

"Well, you didn't go wrong on breakfast," Mateo said, positioning himself under the banyan tree so that, like Lizzie, he could sit and watch the ocean as morning turned into noon.

"You have to watch the portions, though. The food is good and the portions are huge. I usually take enough back with me for another meal or two."

She settled in next to Mateo, too full to move, too early in the day to feel so relaxed. But she was, and it felt good.

"So, tell me about moving to the States," she asked. "Was it traumatic? Because even as many times as I moved with my dad, it just seemed routine."

"After we moved to the States, when I didn't speak a word of English, I would hang around this little grocery store for hours—listening to conversations, trying to pick up the language. And I'd ask questions of anybody who paid the least little bit of attention to me. My school classes were taught in English, so I was getting the education I really needed at the store. In fact, I was there so much the owner gave me a job, sweeping the floors and stocking the shelves. He paid me very little, but he taught me to speak English and speak it properly. It's not easy when the first words you can understand and can speak are the names of various vegetables, but to this day I can pronounce rutabaga better than anyone."

"Have you ever eaten one?" she asked lightly.

"Hell, no. Those things are nasty." He faked a huge cringe.

"Well, finally we agree on something."

"We could agree on something else if you like," he said.

"And what would that be?" she asked.

"That today's a perfect day to walk along the shore, maybe even go wading, but not alone."

"You're a man of vast differences, Mateo. So, tell me… How is taking a walk with you going to make a difference for me?"

"You're tough, Lizzie," he said, taking hold of her hand and helping her off the ground, so she could take her glass back to the bar for a refill of the *lilikoi* juice. "But so am I—and that's what I want to talk about."

And talk quickly, before he backed out. Because his plan was a hard-set plan that she might like or might hate. He wanted to do this immediately, before negative energy zapped him of this little burst of courage. Now or never.

And that worried him, because his life nowadays was closer to the never…

\* \* \*

She loved to walk along the shoreline at any time of the day or night. It was a quiet place, a peaceful place. Sometimes, after her dad was asleep, she'd used to slip away for a few minutes and go stand on the shore, or maybe walk into the water until it was up to her knees and simply take in the beauty of the night.

It had been the only time she'd felt in control. During the day, as often as not, her job had kept her off-balance, due to so many different and difficult demands. And as evenings went, the routine had never changed. She'd sit with her dad in the garden for a while as he fussed with the flowers—something he did even when his memory was practically gone. Then she'd fix his dinner, get him ready for bed, and finally tuck him in.

Most nights she'd sit in the hall on the floor outside his door for an hour, hoping he was sleeping. Sometimes he was, sometimes he wasn't. Those were the nights he'd get up and wander, and she'd go after him, and then they'd start the whole evening routine over, because he wouldn't remember he'd already done it once and demand to do it again. Including eating dinner.

Some people had told her locking him in his room would be for his own good. But he was her dad and he hadn't deserved that. She could have hired someone to sit with him at night, but so much of her life had already been disrupted, and she hadn't wanted more of it going by the wayside. So she'd done whatever the circumstances had called for. She'd sat outside his door...sometimes slept outside his door.

Slipping out and going to the water's edge had been a rare and guilty pleasure, because even though she'd gone there to relax one eye had always been on the house.

"So why the walk?" she asked Mateo, as they came to a stop and he bent to slip off her sandals.

"Want to go wading with me?"

The truth was, she did. But after kissing him she was afraid that anything even remotely resembling something romantic would bring about consequences far greater than she knew.

She was attracted to him. But she was also afraid of involvement. There'd never been a relationship in her life that had gone the way she'd thought it would, and while she was well able to wade in shallow water, nothing about Mateo signaled shallow water at all.

"What if I don't want to?" she asked, half hoping he would drag her into the water.

Something like that would be new to her, and being captured by Mateo... Yes, she liked the idea of that. Captured, carried, conquered... All pure fantasy, of course. But nice when it involved Mateo.

"I'm strong enough to carry you."

"You have a twenty-five-pound lifting restriction for a while yet," she answered, wondering why she was protesting so adamantly when part of her really wanted it.

"You're not my doctor, remember? You're just the person I'm living with presently. And telling the person I'm living with that they have a lifting restriction—well...it's something I'd never do. So, in theory, that's information you don't have."

Despite her attempt to stay serious, Lizzie laughed. "I wish I knew what kind of personality you used to have, because I like this one."

"And if it turns out to be the other one? Or one we haven't met at all? Then what?" He kicked off his shoes and headed toward her. "Tell me, Lizzie. Then what?"

"Then we deal with what we're given."

"But what if all my personalities are just part of me, and when you piece them together it turns me into who I really am?"

"Maybe I already like who I'm seeing."

"Seriously?"

"I don't judge people, Mateo. I accept them as they are. Or in some cases don't accept them."

"And you accept me as I am? Even though I'm not sure that person can really be defined yet?"

"Oh, I think there's a lot of definition stacking up. You're just not ready to deal with it yet."

"You know what they say: to everything there is a season…"

"The fine art of procrastination. It can become habitual, Mateo. Just saying…'"

She smiled, then headed toward the water, but Mateo beat her to it, grabbing hold of her hand and pulling her all the way in.

"No procrastination in this," he said, as her

head bobbed above the water. "I wanted to do it and I did it."

She splashed water in his face, then started to pull away from him, but he caught her by the hand and held her there, the water just barely touching her shoulders.

"I want to find myself, Lizzie, and I can't do it alone. But it scares me to think how deep I could drag you in."

"Only as deep as I want to go, Mateo. You can't pull me any harder than I let you."

"I was just looking for a place to stay for a few nights, and now this is beginning to sound like a commitment."

"Nothing wrong with commitments. We make them and live with them every day. Should I get out of bed this morning? Coffee or tea with my breakfast? The blue shirt or the white one? Should I let a virtual stranger stay in my *ohana* or let him wander around lost and hope he makes it? We make our choices and those turn into commitments. No, I'm not getting out of bed this morning. I'm committed to staying in bed. And I want to wear the blue shirt while I'm drinking my coffee. Commitment, commitment."

"What about the man sleeping in your *ohana*? Commitment there, as well?"

"Yes, but I haven't figured out what kind."

She wasn't sure she wanted to figure it out. Her dad had always accused her of being too tenderhearted, like that was a bad thing. But it was part of her...the part that opened her up to getting hurt. Like marrying the wrong man because he told her the right story. So her commitment to Mateo—it had to be what worked for him, but also what worked for her. Problem was, she didn't know what worked for her anymore.

"So, let's start this commitment with you doing the cooking while I clean up after you. And you can tend the flowers since I don't have a green thumb."

"And this is part of your treatment plan?"

"It's called retraining yourself to be disciplined. It's where you start, and I'll add things as I see fit."

"It's also called being your slave."

"That, too," she said, smiling. "Also, what about cars? Are you a good mechanic?"

That one stumped him for a moment, and he frowned. Then he shut his eyes. It was interesting watching him search for a memory, and in her experience, when something triggered someone as her simple question had triggered Mateo, there was usually a morsel there. So she stood thigh-high in the surf and watched the outward signs of his inward battle for a couple of minutes before he finally sighed, then smiled.

"I had a…a… Damn, it was a 1957 Bel-Air. Convertible. Red."

He shut his eyes again and didn't open them as he struggled to find more of the memory. She could see there was more coming back to him, and he was smiling as it returned, which excited her.

"A classic?" she asked, to prompt him back into the moment.

"It was. I found it in an old storage warehouse in pieces. The owner said I could have it."

Suddenly, he opened his eyes and looked at her.

"I remember this, Lizzie. Remember it like it just happened. The deal was I locked up for him… Old Man McMichaels—we called him Mick. I made a deal with Mick to lock up for him every night so he could get home early to his wife and kids. If I wanted to lock myself in and work on the car that was OK with him. And if I sold the car he got half. Except I didn't sell the car. It's… I think it's still in his warehouse. Or could be. He said he'd keep it for me until I came back for it. It runs perfectly. At least it did. And it's the only car I've ever had."

He looked at her and a puzzled expression came over him.

"I didn't remember that before, Lizzie. Why is that something I would have forgotten?

"Even the experts can't explain the workings of the brain. And keep in mind that the farther away you get from your accident and surgery, the better you'll do."

"It does work in mysterious ways," he said. "Sometimes when I was a field surgeon I'd see a brain injury so bad I didn't think there was any hope for recovery, and then recovery was almost instantaneous. Then other times…"

He shut his eyes again. Then shook his head.

"He wanted an aspirin. That's why he'd come in that day. Had a headache. Asked for an aspirin. Died before I could give it to him." He opened his eyes and stared at her for a moment. "I hated brain trauma. Hated what I could see, hated what I couldn't."

"Did you have many patients with brain injuries?"

"Too many," he said. "I'm a… I *was* a general surgeon. I had no business doing neurosurgery. But sometimes it couldn't be helped, if we couldn't get a neurosurgeon in for whatever reason." He sighed heavily. "And look where I ended up. Life can sure play some messed-up tricks, can't it?"

Turning slowly, he looked directly into her eyes.

"But you already know that, don't you?"

"Meaning?"

"Your father. Brilliant surgeon, the way you tell it. Then…" He shrugged. "Did he know, Lizzie? Did he know what was happening to him?"

"At first. And he fought back—a lot like the way you do. With stubbornness and resistance. But as his illness progressed, and more of him got lost, the knowledge of what was happening to him went away as well, taking all those years of bravery and the good things he'd done.

That was the worst part, I think. Watching this giant of a man lose the things that had made him a giant. He earned those memories and he deserved to have them. But there was nothing I could do except tell him about the things he'd done. And to him they were just stories. Something that kept him entertained for a little while. But even that stage didn't last long, so after that went away I showed him pictures. They meant nothing to him, though. He didn't even recognize himself."

She swatted back a tear sliding down her face.

"It isn't fair, Mateo. Not to him, not to you, not to anybody. Losing yourself like that…" She shook her head. "But you've got hope. My dad had none and there was nothing I could do about that, even though I tried."

"Did you ever resent him for what you had to do?"

"Sometimes…a little. I think it's natural when the demands become more and more. But in a real sense…no. It wasn't his fault."

"And you: the healer who couldn't fix the person you loved the most." He pulled her into his arms and held her there as the water lapped around them. "I'm sorry you had to go through that, Lizzie. It can't have been easy, and there's nothing else to say except I wish it could have been different for you."

"Like you said, life can sure play some messed-up tricks."

"Why here? Why did you bring him here? Was it just because of the flowers?"

"It was so that a practitioner by the name of Malana Palakiko could treat him. She's a holistic practitioner who uses light therapy, acupuncture, and natural herbs. Traditional medicine had run its course and I'm…open-minded. She has a little clinic a few miles from here, and since nothing else was working… She's one of the best when it comes to treating various forms of dementia. And, while she can't cure Alzheimer's, she does make her patients feel better, and she's had some good results in prolonging the inevitable. Dad loved seeing her. The thing was, even while I knew there wasn't any good outcome, I wanted to make his life as good as it could be as he was fading away, and I think Malana did that. She was so…kind. Patient. Understanding."

"And his doctors at the hospital?"

"When a case is hopeless, sometimes their efforts are as much for the loved one as for the patient."

"Was it that way for you?"

"Maybe. I just wanted to do everything I could. He would have expected that from me. But so much of his treatment… I think it was designed to make *me* feel better, like I was really doing something good for him. What *was* good for him, though, was sitting in the garden and tending his flowers. I didn't see that at first. I was so busy pushing him into treatments that weren't working." She laid her head against his chest. "I could have done better for him."

"Something tells me you're being too hard on yourself."

"Or not hard enough. I knew he was going to be a huge responsibility and I was willing to make sacrifices. What I wasn't willing to do was find support for myself—and it's out there. I'm not the only one to have done what I did, and if I'd just listened—" Her voice broke and she quit talking.

"Is that why you want to help me, Lizzie?

To make up for what you feel you didn't do for your dad?"

That thought had never occurred to her, and she was so startled by it she stepped away from Mateo. "Is that what you think?"

"I'm not sure what I think, to be honest. I know your intention isn't malicious, but…"

"But it might be self-serving?"

"People aren't often as generous and kind as you are. In my experience, there's always a motive. People helped me along because I was a boy with brown skin who had an unlimited future ahead of me. Give me an extra shove and you can claim some of that feel-good motive for yourself."

"That's not me, Mateo. People in my life didn't have motives. In fact, I was hardly ever noticed. As for trying to have a feel-good moment at your expense…" She shook her head vehemently. "I don't know what it takes to gain your trust, but I don't come bundled in motives. My life is a lot simpler than that."

"There's nothing simple about you, Lizzie. Nothing at all. Maybe that's why I'm falling… why I like you so much. You're complicated, yet guileless, and the two put together are an interesting mix."

"How interesting?" she asked.

"Very interesting," he replied as he pulled her back to him and lowered his head to kiss her. "Maybe the most interesting person I've ever met—even if I'm not sure how many people I've met and which ones I considered interesting."

"If you intend on kissing me now's the time, Mateo. Unless you'd rather keep on talking and talking and talking..."

Even in the near darkness of the evening he could see her sadness. Or maybe it was more that he could feel it. He understood the melancholia that came with the darkening of the day. Remembered it from Afghanistan, listening to the moans and cries in the night coming from his ward. People in so much pain and fear and he couldn't fix them. Some who would never go home. Some who would.

And now there was his own irrational fear of the dark. During the day he could be as belligerent as hell, and blowing off his anger that way worked. But when it turned dark his belligerence disappeared, to be replaced by melancholia and fear. And some of those moans and some of those cries in the night had been his.

And probably Lizzie's as well. Strangely, that hurt him maybe even more than his own pain did—knowing that something far deeper than she would let him know about was pulling her in.

"Care for a swim?" he asked, for the lack of anything better to say.

"I'm always in the mood for a swim," she said.

After the kiss they'd returned to the house and changed into beach clothes, and taken a towel along with them. Now he grabbed her up off the towel and carried her to the water—where he dropped her.

He didn't set her down gently. Didn't even give her the option to go wading. Against her lame protests he carried her out until he was waist-deep, then dropped her. She went under for a second, and when she popped back up she grabbed his hand and pulled him down with her.

"You could be risking my life," he said, laughing.

Her response was to splash him, then dive back under before he could retaliate. But he was strong in the water. As he dived down he grabbed her by the arm and pulled her back up to the surface, then splashed her the way she'd done him.

"Apparently I have some skill at this," he said, then dove back under.

This time when he surfaced he was about twenty yards away from where they'd been before, and he didn't see her.

"Lizzie?" he called, turning around in circles and looking for signs of her. "This isn't funny, Lizzie. Where are you?"

Her answer was to grab him by the ankle and pull him under, then get away before he had time to resurface. Except he'd already antici-pated she'd do something like that, so he got himself all the way down to the sandy ocean floor, then grabbed her ankle and pulled her down on top of him. *Fully* on top of him.

He held her there for a moment, before he re-alized he was enjoying not only the playtime but the feel of his body against hers entirely too much. So he pointed up, then released her, and followed her to the surface. Both came up spitting out water and laughing.

"Just wait until I get you on a bodyboard," she warned him, and she shoved back the hair from her face enough to see that he was staring at her. Up close and personal. Staring with such an intent look that it gave her shivers that were visible to him.

He hadn't meant to. But she was so beautiful he couldn't help himself. Whether or not she was a woman he would have chosen before, he had no clue. But if he were able to choose now, the only woman in his mind was Lizzie.

That was the problem. There might be other things in his mind that would dictate different choices. And even if there weren't she didn't deserve his problems. As a friend, he appreciated her willingness to help. But as anything else...

"Don't know if I've ever been surfing, or bodyboarding, but the sooner the better," he growled, trying to take those other things off his mind.

And then he dove down and headed underwater for the beach, carrying with him feelings for Lizzie that were far deeper than anything he'd intended.

Was he falling in love? Despite his attempts to talk himself out of it, and all the rationalizations that he didn't want or need that in his life—especially now—was that what was happening to him?

Lizzie headed to the shore as well, wondering when fifteen feet had turned into such a long journey. But it was, and by the time she'd managed to make it to shore Mateo was already standing there in ankle-deep water, dripping wet and looking sexier than any man had a right to—in the dark, in the light, or any other shading of the day.

*What am I doing?* she asked herself as she stood and walked back to the sand, taking care to keep her eyes averted. *And why am I doing it?*

Because she was attracted to him, pure and simple. She was an adult. There was nothing stopping her. Except common sense. And right now, try as she might, she couldn't dredge it up.

So as she walked past him she turned her

head to avoid temptation, and words she hadn't intended to say slipped out. "You look good in the water."

"I wasn't sure you'd noticed."

"Oh, I notice. But I don't always react."

"Sounds very military to me."

"It probably is. My dad always told me to keep my emotions inside, said that people didn't want to see them. When I did, he called me his brave little soldier, and that was high praise coming from a man who didn't believe in coddling anyone."

"So when you said you'd noticed me..."

"The way any woman would notice a good-looking man. I'm only human, Mateo. Maybe a bit more reserved than you're used to, but I'm normal in all the ways that count." She reached over and brushed his cheek with her hand. "This living arrangement could get difficult because of that. But there are worse things in life than being attracted to a good-looking man."

"Or woman," he replied.

"So if we know it's there between us it becomes easier. At least, it should."

After only a few days, Lizzie was already

starting to like having someone there with her. Or was it Mateo she liked having there? Either way, this past year had been so lonely, and having a little noise around the house other than her own was nice. Especially after that kiss…

"Are you sure that's true?" he asked, walking alongside her, but at a safe distance. "Admit an attraction and then hope it can be held at an arm's length?"

"I'm not sure how we're supposed to work. More than that, I'm not sure I know how I *want* us to work. Friends, partners, lov—"

She didn't finish the sentence because this was becoming too deep, and she didn't want a volley of emotions going back and forth between them. Especially when there was every possibility that her feelings were turning into more than she'd expected. He was easy to like, she was discovering. More than that, if she allowed herself to admit it, he would also be easy to love—even with parts of him missing.

But could she go through that again? That was the question she needed to figure out before she took the wrong step. Because she did know what it was like living with someone who was fragmented. It was difficult, sad, tedious, and moments of joy were so few and far between.

But that had been her dad. Not Mateo. Which led her to an even bigger question. Could she separate the two? There were similarities in their problems, although not that many. And Mateo was caring and warm while her dad had not been. Still, she'd loved her dad because he'd tried to do better. Yet in her mind the similarities were still large. And that was what scared her.

Would there ever be a time when Mateo occupied all her thoughts, as well as her whole heart, and didn't get squeezed out?

"Like I said before, Lizzie, you can tell me to leave anytime. No explanation necessary."

"I know I can." But she wanted him there. Liked having him there. He balanced her out while she went through her own ups and downs and never judged or asked questions. "That's not what I want."

"Meaning you like having me here?"

"I do, Mateo. It's sort of out of character for me, but yes, I like having you here."

He smiled as he watched her make her way to the front door. She wasn't easy. In fact in a lot of ways, she was difficult. But he liked being here with her, too. In fact, he could see that feeling growing the longer he stayed. She wasn't orthodox, she wasn't predictable, but Lizzie was the real deal, and he was attracted to that asset almost as much as he was to her *other* assets.

"Time will tell," he said aloud, as he walked around to the *ohana*. Time and, he hoped, a few more pieces of his memory.

*"You need to go up there, Doc. He's bad and he'll stand a better chance with you."*

*"I'm not supposed to do this."*

*Sweat was dripping off his brow, yet he was chilled to the bone. Looking up, he saw the two medics up there working frantically. And they were looking down at him, expecting him to trade places.*

*"You got an IV in?" he yelled up to them, but his voice didn't carry over the sound of the gunfire that was much closer than he cared to admit. "IV!" he shouted. "Get an IV in him."*

*They had the equipment with them, and it would be easier for them to use it than for him to carry up more than he had to.*

*"Get the IV in him, then I'll come up."*

*Which meant one of them would come down, since the watchtower platform was too small to hold three people, let alone four.*

*"IV!" he shouted again, indicating the vein in his left forearm.*

*Finally one of them leaned over and shouted. "Don't come up, Doc. Too risky. We'll get him down to you, then you can—"*

*As he was shouting a shot rang out, hitting the soldier in what appeared to be his chest.*

*"What do we do, Doc?" one of the men on the ground asked. "Tell me what to do!"*

*Then suddenly they were dying.*

*They were all dying.*

*"I don't know!" Mateo screamed. "I don't know."*

*When he looked up again it was Freddy hanging over the edge. Freddy with his chest ripped open. His friend. His only friend out here.*

As he screamed, he woke up in a puddle of sweat. The bedsheets were drenched and his hands were shaking. His memory was returning, and he wasn't sure he wanted it to. What had happened that night…none of it was good. None of it.

Sighing, Mateo left the bed and walked to the window, opened it, and looked out at the stars for a little while.

It wasn't going to leave him. Other things had. Too many things. But this? This was hanging on in huge chunks, tormenting him.

Some memories weren't meant to be remembered and this was one of them. But it was coming back. Damn it. It was coming back.

His screams carried through the night and she couldn't run fast enough to get to him.

"Mateo," she choked, barely slowing as she ran through the front door and up the stairs to his room.

He was standing at the window. Staring out. Not moving. Barely breathing.

"Tell me what to do."

He turned slowly to face her. "They all died, Lizzie. Every one of them, including Freddy. And I was the only one who—" His voice broke, and he sank to the floor. "There was nothing I could do to help any of them."

Lizzie sat on the floor next to him, putting

her arm around his shoulder even though he was stiff and resistant. "I'm ready to listen if you're ready to talk."

"But there's nothing to say. I took a risk. Went up the tower when I should have waited. Drew enemy fire and got every one of my ground support killed."

There were so many things she wanted to say—most of them trite. But he didn't need that. So instead she pulled him a little closer and sat quietly, waiting for him to speak again.

It was nearly five minutes before he did.

"Nobody came for a couple of days. The whole area was under heavy fire and they had no idea that one of the casualties was alive. So I lay there, going in and out of consciousness, and I have no idea when I was rescued or what happened after that. The next thing I remember is waking up in Germany. I'd had surgery—I remember that. But I didn't remember my name. Not for days. Or maybe weeks. Then I was sent Stateside, and you know the rest. Belligerent patient. Refuses to help himself."

"Survivor's remorse?" she asked.

"Probably."

Now it was beginning to make sense to her. Mateo was beginning to make sense to her. He didn't want to get better because somewhere, buried deep, he believed he should have died with his men. This wasn't about his memory loss, or his hatred of being a patient. It was about the very essence of a man who carried a burden he didn't deserve.

"Why now?" she asked. "What's bringing all this back now?"

She feared it was something she was doing, or not doing, and she wanted to know.

"Maybe because I feel safe here. The truth is, it's never clear why something surfaces when it does. That's something they've been telling me since Germany. No one really knows why something happens when it does."

"I like the explanation that you feel safe."

"So do I," he said.

# CHAPTER SEVEN

BEFORE MATEO, BREAKFAST had always been quick. If she ate it, she never lingered. Most often she grabbed a coffee on the way to work and didn't think about food until her belly told her she was hungry. If it didn't, as often as not she didn't eat.

But this morning she felt like making breakfast for Mateo the way he'd done for her these past mornings. It was simple. Nothing like his elaborate spread. Fresh fruit, toast. And in the casualness of the moment she felt relaxed. Relaxed enough to ask his opinion.

So, over her second cup of coffee, she told him about her opportunity to move from the hospital to a private practice as a primary care provider. She knew it was something her dad would have dismissed as stupid before she'd have been able to get all the words out. He'd actually told her so before his Alzheimer's got so bad.

"Kahawai is really pressuring me. He wants me to buy out his uncle's small practice, possibly expand it, and treat the people who live in the area. He's put me on a deadline now. Says he's going after you if I don't accept."

"Are you happy at the hospital?"

"I'm not *un*happy. It's just that there are so many memories here I'm not sure I want to stay. Not sure I want to go, either."

"Do you have other options?" he asked.

"A few. None that excite me, though. Maybe I'm too picky—or maybe I'm in a place where I shouldn't be making major life decisions yet. Whatever the case, I won't be doing anything without good reason. So, are you up for a body-boarding lesson today?"

"The best possible scenario is that once I paddle out into the water it all comes back to me and I remember all the medals I won as a world-class surfer."

Lizzie laughed. "I don't recall your name being on any medal list. Which championship was it?"

"See, that's where amnesia comes in handy. All I have to do is say I don't remember, and people won't press for more information. They'll just assume I'm what I claim to be."

"Have you ever surfed, Mateo?"

"Not to my knowledge," he said seriously.

"Well, it's too soon after your head surgery to do anything more than paddle on your stomach. And, while I already know the reaction I'm going to get, I think you should wear a helmet."

"A stylish one, I hope?" he said, taking both their coffee cups to the sink, then rinsing them out before they went into the dishwasher. "If all I'm allowed is bodyboarding, I'll accept that. But the helmet's got to be pretty damned cool."

"Because...?" she asked, biting back her smile.

"Because I'm pretty damned cool, and I don't want my reputation ruined by a helmet."

She liked that little bit of stubbornness in him. It was sexy. But was it really him? And was she always bound to wonder if things were really him?

"Then we'll get you a cool helmet. Pink, purple, neon-green?"

"Black—with stripes. Maybe red stripes. And all the gear to match."

He was really quite funny when he wanted to be, and she enjoyed that, because she needed some lightness in her life. "Whatever you say."

"What if I say that you make me nervous?"

"I'll ask you why, and you'll probably come up with some good lie I'll believe."

"Except I'd never lie to you. Not intention-ally."

And just like that the light moment had turned serious.

"I may not be the me who existed before, but no matter who I am I'd never lie to you." He reached out and held her face between his hands. "Your face and especially your eyes are very expressive, Lizzie Peterson. Your eyes would show if you ever lied to me. But you wouldn't do that."

"Are you that sure of me?" she asked, back-ing away from him. His touch was too real, and it was a reality she didn't want to face.

"What if I said yes? That I trust you more than anyone else I've ever trusted except for my mother?"

"I'm not sure what I've done to earn that, but I'd be flattered."

"Then be prepared to be flattered, because I do." He bent to her ear and whispered, "And I think I always will."

She wanted desperately to ask him what he meant by that, but she was afraid of the answer. She'd said yes to a man once before, then proceeded directly into hell. And, while Mateo was nothing at all like Brad, she wondered about her judgment. Maybe didn't trust it so much. Or perhaps everything stemmed from her need not to be alone.

Whatever the case, she wasn't prepared to give Mateo an answer to the question she was pretty sure was coming. So she backed away from him.

"Give me half an hour, then we'll meet in the garden and go rent a couple of bodyboards. We have one quick stop to make first. I promised Kahawai I'd look at the clinic."

"So you *are* giving it some thought?"

"Maybe a little. I'm not one to shut down my options the way—"

She stopped. Mateo was his own man and

he was going to do what he wanted to do. At least until he believed that asking for real help was a good option. If that ever happened.

"The way I am?" he asked. "That's what you were going to say, isn't it?"

"Let's just say we're not alike."

"But opposites attract, don't they?"

And they *were* opposites in so many ways. Yet they were also so much alike.

"Who said anything about attracting? All I did was mention I wanted to go look at the clinic. You're welcome to come, or you can do whatever you want. It's your choice," she said.

In so many ways, everything was his choice. But she wasn't sure he was ready for all the choices that would come his way.

Time would tell, she supposed.

The clinic was bustling when Lizzie and Mateo entered. The line was long, but nobody seemed put out by the wait. It was staffed by one elderly doctor, who didn't move fast, one medical assistant, and one receptionist. People had brought their lunches and were spread out in the garden outside, eating.

It seemed more like a social gathering place than a medical office, and Mateo liked the feel of that. It wasn't the way he practiced, but he could see Lizzie here, working at a different pace than she normally did, and being happy doing it.

"It's not what I expected," he said, as they made their way through the waiting room to the back, where Doc Akoni looked exhausted as he went from one exam room to the another.

"Two doctors here would be great," he said, assuming Mateo was here to enquire along with Lizzie. "The practice is booming, but I'm too old to keep up with it. My goal is to spend the rest of my years with my wife and do the things we never had time to do before. You know...visit kids and grandkids. Travel... Live out my life in leisure."

"Where do your emergency patients go?" Mateo asked, looking over some of the outdated equipment that was still in use: a breathing machine, an X-ray rig, something that chugged along doing rudimentary blood tests, and a few other gadgets that looked as old as he was.

"There are a couple of hospitals with good

emergency care down the coast, if the situation isn't too urgent. And, of course, we can air transport them down to Honolulu when it's necessary."

"How often is that?" Lizzie asked.

"More often than I care for. There are some good clinics in the area, but as far as hospital beds go nothing much around here."

"What about Malakapua Pointe?" asked Mateo.

Lizzie shook her head. "No emergency department. That was never part of the plan."

Doc Akoni escorted his next patient into one of the three exam rooms. "Janis Lawton had her vision for Malakapua when it was being built here," he explained. "And, while we were hoping for some kind of emergency department, she was very specific as to the kind of patient she wanted. Her general care wards and surgeries don't really lend themselves to a broader base of patients with the kinds of injuries and illnesses you see here in this clinic. We're minor. We treat the little things and make referrals for patients who need more than we offer. Nobody comes here expecting open heart surgery, or even an appendectomy."

"Which makes you a country doctor," Mateo said.

He was looking at the little girl who was the next patient in the queue. Her skin was red and blistering. She looked listless and dizzy. And it was clear she was suffering with nausea. Definite signs of sun poisoning.

"Can I help you out with your next patient?"

"You can see all the patients you want. I'm assuming you're the doc everybody's talking about...the one with amnesia?"

"Amnesia in some areas. But many parts of my life are intact—like the part that sees a clear case of sun poisoning."

"You know enough to ask for help if you need it, don't you?" Akoni asked.

Mateo nodded.

"And you can read an X-ray? Because we have a rather outdated machine."

Mateo nodded again.

"Sutures?"

"Yes. I can put in sutures."

"Then it sounds to me like you're good to go. Lab coats are in the back, along with an extra stethoscope. There's one central area for supplies, which I keep locked. We don't dispense medicine because the salesmen prefer to avoid us, meaning no free samples. Also, because we're not a pharmacy, we're not licensed to prescribe. Oh, and don't try to refer patients to…" he nodded sideways at Lizzie "…to *her* hospital. Like I said, they don't do trauma, or any sort of emergency, and there's hell to pay if one of our patients accidentally ends up there. The other places we use are much nicer."

Lizzie raised her eyebrows at his pronouncement. She'd heard him say as much before, but didn't really believe it was that bad. But maybe it was. Maybe it was something she should check into if she went back.

"So, how will you treat her?" she asked Mateo, referring to the child.

"Cool compresses. A lot of fluids. And if that doesn't bring up her hydration level fast enough, an IV. Treat her nausea. Take care of her skin with some kind of medicated moisturizer. And keep her out of the sun for a while. Bed rest for a couple of days if she comes down with a fever or chills, which is likely. Then ibuprofen for that. It's all pretty basic.

Nothing to worry about that general care won't take care of."

"You're good," Lizzie commented, genuinely impressed.

"So, for now," said Doc Akoni, "if you need to prescribe any real treatment, and not simply apply a bandage, why don't you run it by me first? Or Lizzie, if she cares to stay. All things considered, I don't think you need close supervision at this level of care, but just to be safe…"

"Not a problem," Mateo said. "It's just like going through my residency again."

"Well, be patient. Things will change," said Doc Akoni.

Mateo nodded, then took the child by her hand and led her toward the exam room, motioning for her mother to follow.

"I could use someone like you around here," said Doc Akoni, on his way into exam room one.

"Even with my condition?" Mateo asked, looking at the old-fashioned whiteboard hanging on the reception area wall, where patients signed their names as they came through the door.

"Even with your condition. If you didn't lose your general skills, this could all be yours."

"Not sure I'm ready to run a clinic on my own. Even one as basic as this."

"Things change, son. You never know who might be standing right behind you, eager to help. All I'm saying is, don't discount yourself. You've got everything you need to do this job, if you set yourself free to do it."

Mateo glanced at Lizzie, who was busy talking to a woman who was obviously well along in her pregnancy. "Mind if I hang around here for a little while and help?" he asked her. "Maybe put the bodyboarding off until later this afternoon?"

He nodded down toward the woman's swollen ankles, and Lizzie acknowledged his discovery with a wink.

"I think helping out would be a good way to spend the morning. Maybe I'll stay and put in a few hours as well. And the first thing... Would you mind consulting with me, Dr. Sanchez? My patient is nearing her thirtieth week, and the edema in her feet and ankles is indeed what's bothering her. Since I haven't worked a maternity case in years..."

Mateo looked at the woman's name on the whiteboard, then found a paper file in a rickety old filing cabinet. He studied it for a moment, then nodded. "Why don't you make Leilani comfortable in exam room two, since it's open? I'll be in shortly."

"You OK?" Lizzie whispered as she passed by him on her way into exam two. "Can you handle maternity? I know it's a little more than first aid, but…"

"I did it when I was overseas. A lot of the women who lived there depended on us."

"Then you're the man for the job."

"Only if you oversee what I'm doing. I'm not ready to fly solo with anything more than a cut or a bruise."

"Or CPR," she reminded him as she entered the exam room.

That was true. And so many things had come back to him—like why Leilani had swollen ankles. It wasn't part of the scope of a surgeon's responsibility, but he knew. It was coming back to him. All the pregnant women he'd treated in Afghanistan. The complications… the normal but uncomfortable things. It made him nervous and excited at the same time.

* * *

Lizzie wasn't sure what Mateo was thinking, and she hadn't intended working here for any part of the day, but Mateo's eyes sparkled with happiness and excitement.

That didn't mean he was finding himself, but it could mean he was finding a new place. But here? In this clinic? Or maybe just in the general practice of medicine?

He certainly was good. Quick. Alert. In tune with the details of his patient. It was the first time he'd showed any kind of hope, and she was glad for that. Glad for him. Actually, she felt so excited that if she were twenty years younger, she might be jumping up and down like an eager child.

Twenty minutes after his examination of Leilani, Mateo said, "Everything looks good. Your blood pressure is normal, baby is the right size, and you look like a first-time mom with a glow."

"What about my swollen feet?" she asked.

"Right…" he said, nodding. "It's called edema, and it's normal—especially in the evening and during warmer weather. It happens in about seventy-five percent of all pregnancies, and once it starts you're stuck with it until you deliver."

"Why?" she asked, and her attention was focused solely on Mateo, not Lizzie, who stood off in the corner, observing.

"Well, it happens when your body fluids increase to nurture both you and your baby. That results in increased blood flow and pressure on your expanding uterus, which is what causes the swelling. Look for it to happen in your hands, as well.

"Then it's really normal?" the young woman asked.

"Perfectly—as long as it's kept under control. However, if it becomes excessive, and comes along with a couple of other things, like increased blood pressure or rapid weight gain, that could indicate a problem, and you'll have to let your doctor know about it."

"Is there anything I can do about it? Maybe take a pill, or something?"

"I think the natural things you can do are better. Such as trying not to stay in one position for a long period of time. Also, elevate your legs when you're sitting. And I always recommend sleeping on your side—your left side—because it helps your kidneys eliminate waste, which reduces swelling. Then, there are other things that might help. Pregnancy-appropriate exercising. Avoiding tight socks or stockings. Drinking lots of water—around ten glasses a day. That helps eliminate the waste in your system that causes the swelling. And comfy shoes. If they feel good, wear them—and skip the vanity shoes. And, last but not least, cut out excess salt. It causes you to retain water, which is exactly what you don't want."

"It sounds so simple," Leilani said, heading toward the exam room door.

"It is—and it will only last a few more months." Mateo smiled as he escorted Leilani through to the waiting room. "Just use common sense and you'll be fine. But if you think something's not right call a doctor—or a nurse practitioner, if that's who you're using."

"I'm not using anybody," she said. "Doc Akoni confirmed my pregnancy at the beginning, but now when I come here and see so many people waiting I don't stay, because I have to get back to my job. Today I got lucky. You're here and the line is going faster."

"You need regular care," Mateo told her. "For your own health as well as your baby's."

"I'll get it closer to the time."

With that, Leilani disappeared through the door and hurried on her way.

"She doesn't get any regular care," he said to Lizzie, who was standing in the hallway, still watching him.

"A lot of people don't. I saw it when I traveled with my dad. See it here, too. Too many complaints…not enough doctors to go around."

She was proud of the way he had handled himself, and he couldn't have been more spot-on in his examination and in answering Leilani's questions if he'd been an obstetrician.

What Mateo had was a real gift. He remembered things she'd forgotten. Sleeping on your left side—she wasn't sure that was something she'd ever known about pregnancy. She admired what he was doing, looking at something that was new to him, and safe.

Admiring him personally was not so safe. But one was spilling over into the other and she wasn't sure she knew how to stop it.

Or if she even wanted to.

* * *

When the morning was over, and the queue was cut down by more than half, thanks to Lizzie and Mateo pitching in, they decided to postpone their bodyboarding and spend the rest of the afternoon relaxing.

Mateo was glad of that. His headache was back—probably from overexertion. It had been a good long time since he'd worked, and he'd discovered he wasn't in the same good shape he'd used to be when...

Mateo shut his eyes for a moment and fractured pieces of his makeshift military surgery came back to him. Nothing was concrete. Nothing really rang a bell. Except an older nurse sitting at the triage desk... Was she knitting?

"Something wrong?" Lizzie asked as his eyes shot back open.

"Her name was Mary. She knitted...for a grandchild, I think. She was my surgical nurse. Damned good nurse. Knew more than pretty much all the rest of us put together."

"That's just coming back to you?"

He nodded as they took a seat at The Shack, on a lava rock wall surrounding an almond tree. "She was this amazing bundle of energy we all respected. Short, a little round, gray hair, and she could out-move any one of us."

"That's a good sign, Mateo."

"But triggered by what?"

"Something familiar—like working in a congested medical environment this morning. Or something someone said or did. Or maybe one of the patients you treated reminded you of another patient somewhere else? I mean, I don't know enough about triggers to talk about them, but maybe it's just time. Remember: to everything there is a season…?"

They stopped talking as the server brought drinks—lemonade for Lizzie and something Mateo had called "the usual."

"They know you well enough here to bring you a drink without you telling them what you want? I'm impressed."

"It's a mix of fruit juices—whatever's on hand except banana. It overwhelms everything else, so they don't include it."

"And the bartender just happens to remember that?" she asked.

"He was in the clinic earlier. Suffered a pulled muscle in his neck in a minor injury on the beach breakwaters. I just happened to mention what I liked, and I guess he remembered. Care for a sip?" he asked, holding out his tall hurricane glass to her.

"Should I be jealous that you've made friends here already and the only people I know work at the hospital?"

She took the glass and he felt the soft skin of her hand caress his, maybe linger a second or two longer than it should. Their eyes met, again lingering a bit longer than he'd expected. But he wasn't complaining. Being here with Lizzie like this made him realize there was no place else he wanted to be.

Would she ever consider him something more than a friend? Or just a reminder of what had happened to her father? Those were the questions on his mind right now, and he wanted to ask her, but he wouldn't for fear of her answer.

If she said no, that he could never fit into her life in a different way than he already did, that would devastate him. And if she could never look at him without being reminded of her dad's illness… Well, that would be the last piece of sharp-edged glass dropping to the floor...

"Nothing to be jealous of. I've always made friends easily. When I was a kid I could charm just about anybody to get anything I wanted."

"I never really had time to make friends. Just when we were finally settled in one place, it was time to move on. And now... I haven't changed much, to be honest. It's easier being alone. I can make my life exactly what I want it to be without interference."

"I've never really been alone. Growing up, I was social. Then in college and medical school...let's just say I liked to party. After that, the Army wasn't exactly a place where anyone got to be alone."

"My dad was very 'social,' as you call it. But that never happened to me. He always said I wasn't outgoing enough, and as it turns out he was right. I have my work, though."

"And that's enough?"

Lizzie sighed, then took a sip of her lemonade. "Was today enough for *you*, Mateo?"

"It was different—but I can't really judge it in terms of being enough or not enough. I enjoyed the work, enjoyed getting back to medicine for a little while, even if it wasn't in a surgical capacity."

Lizzie was mellow this evening. No particular reason why, but the feeling had been dragging at her most of the day and now she was ready to give in to it. Let it take her wherever it wanted to.

Mateo had gone with a couple of people he'd met at The Shack to a private yacht party, and even though he'd asked her to come along she hadn't been in the mood. Instead she'd stopped by the hospital, to have a chat with Janis, but had decided not to go in once she'd got there.

She and Janis lived the same life. They worked. In twenty years, when she reached the age Janis was now, she could see herself being the one with the tiki cup collection, serving tropical drinks to colleagues who dropped by her office. Tonight, that had just hit too close to home, and she'd decided she didn't want to see it, so instead she'd gone home, turned on some soft music and was now reading the latest volume of *Topics in Primary Care*.

The first article that caught her attention was

about newly approved disease-modifying therapies for multiple sclerosis. It was an expanding field that was resulting in some exciting outcomes. Next she read about Trigeminal Nerve Stimulation for ADHD in children, but wasn't sure that kind of electrical stimulation was anything she wanted to try. Finally, when she got to an article about initiatives in the management of non-motor symptoms in Parkinson disease, her eyes practically crossed.

But she was too tired to go upstairs to bed. So she shut her eyes and allowed herself five minutes to rest there before undertaking the stairs.

It was warm indoors. The fan overhead was spinning, but still moisture dampened the front of Lizzie's floral green Hawaiian wrapdress—her favorite for lounging. She stretched out on the chaise, revealing long, tanned legs underneath the dress, then arched back, hoping to catch a little more of the breeze from the fan.

Five minutes led to ten, which led to twenty, which led to an hour—and all she got for spending the extra time lounging was such a vivid image of Mateo she didn't want to interrupt it.

Perspiration was beading between her breasts now, and it wasn't all about the heat.

"Looks like you're having a restless night," he said, from outside the open lanai door.

"Medical journals make me restless," she said, tugging her dress back into place and assuming a more conversational position. "I didn't think you'd be back this early."

"Parties are boring when you don't know anybody there." He stepped inside but kept his distance, going no farther than just barely in the door. "The people seemed nice enough, but I decided I'd rather come back here and spend the rest of the evening with you."

He gave her legs an obvious stare, then moved a few more steps into the room.

"I thought maybe we could go swimming. No one's down on the beach and it's a lot cooler outside than it is in here. Care to go?" He walked over to her and held out his hand.

She was sure he was staring at her breasts. Her dress did nothing but make them more prominent than they already were. He'd caught her looking a way no one was meant to see, and there was nothing to do about it but ignore the fact that she was barely dressed and either go with him or go to bed.

And while going to bed had seemed appealing an hour ago, she was over that now, and her mind was forming a vision of her and Mateo on the beach.

Bold move...but Mateo made her feel bold. And needy. And ready to try something that would make sure she didn't end up serving drinks in pink ceramic pineapples to anybody who happened to be passing by.

So she took his hand, stood, and followed as he led her out the lanai door, not missing the fact that he was dressed in long cargos and a white dress shirt, and hadn't changed into swimwear.

"We didn't turn on the floodlights," she said, as they headed toward the beach.

"Do we need the light?" he asked, stopping and turning to face her. "There's a big moon out tonight, and that should be enough."

The world seemed dreamlike as she stood there, anticipating something...anything. But it was clear from his lack of movement that the next move was up to her to make—if there were to be a move. So, without speaking, she started to undo the buttons on his shirt. One at a time, as her fingers trembled.

This was uncharted territory for her…seduction. The slow headiness of it. Before, with Brad, it had been an act of urgency on his part and she'd been merely a participant. But this was her seduction, and Mateo made it obvious that to keep going or to stop was for her to decide.

He was watching as she continued to unbutton his shirt, making her way down his chest, taking care to brush her fingers over his skin on her journey. Lizzie liked it that he watched her. It made her feel wanted in a way no man had ever wanted her. So with each button, and each deliberate brush of her fingers to his skin, she went one step more, leaning in to kiss what her fingers had just caressed, and listening to him moan as she did so.

"You know you're killing me," he whispered, as she tugged his shirt off his broad shoulders and dropped it on the ground.

"You know that's what I intend to do," she said, smiling softly at him as his hands reached down and gently caressed her back, her arms, her shoulders.

Then he pulled her up and hard to his chest, letting their heated bodies press together.

"My turn," he said, reciprocating button for button, caress for caress, kiss for kiss, and then likewise pulling her shirt off her shoulders and dropping it on top of his, leaving them pressed together skin to skin.

He was looking into her face. "Did you know this was the first thing I thought about when I met you? You were standing there, arms folded across your chest like you always do, assessing me. And my assessment of you, before I even thought about you as a doctor, was that you completed paradise. I'd taken the standard tour and none of it had made a difference, but then there was you…"

"And *my* first thought was that you were going to be trouble."

"Were you right?"

"In more ways than I counted on."

She let him lead her farther down the path to the beach, and to the edge of the water. That was where they stopped, and she removed his cargos and let him stand there in his boxers.

Would this be the thing that ended them? One more step into the water with Mateo and there would be no turning back. Perhaps somewhere in the deepest part of her she'd known this was inevitable. But what she didn't know was what would come next.

This was where the everyday Lizzie would have stopped. Yet this was where the Lizzie who wanted to come out of her shell would begin. Which was she?

As it turned out, Mateo answered that question with his first kiss. It was soft and delicate, just barely there. Lizzie responded with a second kiss—it was more demanding than she'd expected. Harder than she'd known she *could* kiss.

And that was her answer as she took that next step into the water. Then the next and the next. Even though she couldn't have Mateo in the truest sense, she wanted him *now*, and for the first time in her life Lizzie gave in to what she wanted.

In the ocean.

In the moonlight.

In Mateo's embrace.

## CHAPTER EIGHT

As THE MORNING light peeked in through the blinds Lizzie opened her eyes and stretched, then turned on her side, expecting to see Mateo there. But he was gone.

After their lovemaking in the ocean they'd returned to the house, running bold and naked, not much caring if they were caught, then showered off the sand and spent the rest of the night exploring, then cuddling, and doing all those things that had finally caused her to sleep in his arms, more peaceful and contented than she'd felt in a long, long time.

No promises had been made. In fact, few words had been spoken. There had been no need. Between them, the emotion had been so raw that words hadn't had any place. They'd both known what this was about: a growing need. Still, waking up with him still there would have been nice, and she was disappointed that last night hadn't extended into the morning.

Dressing, then heading downstairs, Lizzie half expected to see Mateo in the kitchen, or maybe on the lanai, but he was in neither place. He'd been there, though. Coffee was made, and there were fresh muffins sitting out, waiting for her.

So she indulged, and by the time she'd finished Mateo was there, standing by the sliding door to the lanai, smiling. He was holding a couple of bodyboards under his arm.

"Are you sure you got the right size?" she asked.

"The girl in the surf shop measured me—twice."

"I'll bet she did," Lizzie said, as she did a mental check to make sure.

The board had to come to about mid-chest, and that was where her eyes fixed for much longer than they should have. But what a chest to fix on...

Having Lizzie stare at him like that was nice, especially after last night. But in the full light of day it made him nervous. It also made him keenly aware that he couldn't have what was within his reach. No delusions, no forgetting anything. She deserved what he couldn't give her—a fully functioning man, not just the shell of someone who didn't know who he was, let alone how he was going to work out the rest of his life.

"You do realize that 'bodyboard' has another meaning, don't you?" he said. "It's used in radiation therapy and it allows the intestinal tract to drop out of the treatment field?"

"You really are full of yourself, aren't you?" she asked, laughing.

"It was just something I remembered when I was buying these. Too bad what came back to me wasn't more useful."

"Well, if that's what you want to use your bodyboard for it's up to you. I prefer to use mine in the water, paddling over the waves…"

"Capsizing?" he asked.

"You always turn toward the negative, don't you?"

He shrugged. "Maybe capsizing is a memory."

"Or maybe it's your way of trying to convince me to let you start with a kneeling board, or even a full surfboard. Which I won't do because you've had brain surgery. In case *that* has slipped your mind."

"Wish it would," he said, resisting the urge to reach up and feel the tiny area where the doctor had drilled. "And it wasn't exactly brain surgery. It's classified as a minimally invasive procedure."

"Like I don't know that?"

"Like there's a huge difference between having part of your skull removed and having a tiny hole drilled."

He knew the procedure like he knew the back of his hand—not because he'd had to remove that many subdural hematomas, but because he'd read up on the procedure dozens of times after it was over. It was so simple—drilling a burr hole the size of a dime, inserting a catheter and letting a clot-buster drug drip in. Over several days the clot disappeared, and there was no need for a more substantial procedure, like a craniotomy, where the skull was cut open and the clot was manually removed.

That was the procedure he'd done too many times, and how he wished he'd known more about the other procedure when he was in the field. But it was still new, and in field surgery the tried and true was always the go-to. He'd been in the hospital in Germany when the procedure had been used on him.

Mateo blinked hard to rid himself of the image of what they'd done to him. It was a reminder of too many things he'd known and done as a battlefield surgeon. Things he'd never be able to do again.

"Nope. Can't forget that. It's caused me to part my hair differently."

"Well, if it's of any consequence, the post-surgical notes I read said your procedure was textbook-perfect."

"Not a comforting thought, Lizzie," he said. "Someone tapping into your brain."

"Because you don't like thinking of yourself as a patient? Or because brain surgery, no matter how minimal, scares the bejeebies out of you, like it does most people?"

"One from Column A and one from Column B, please. Being that close to what could easily have been deadly isn't what I care to have come into my mind. It always does, though. And I know I shouldn't complain, since I was one of the lucky ones, but that doesn't make it any easier."

"Did it ever occur to you that if you start your real recovery by accepting the fact that you were a patient, which makes you the vulnerable one, it might take you to the next step, where you'll start dealing with the emotional aspects of vulnerability? And after that…who knows? But your recovery, Mateo, could take a long time."

"Well, it seems I've got plenty of that," he quipped.

"And in the meantime?"

He shrugged. "Take it a day at a time, I suppose. I mean, what else can I do? And don't suggest anything to do with the hospital, because you know how I feel about that."

"I'm not sure you're aware, but I do listen to the things you say and watch the things you do, and you're not helpless. In fact, you function very well. Like yesterday at the clinic. No mistakes—not even any hesitation. Take note of yourself, Mateo. The answers are there. And if they don't come, then start with something that will make new memories. People do it every day."

"But I'm not 'people,' Lizzie. I'm me, and I'm impatient to get on with my life."

"Then *do* it, Mateo. Starting today—right now—look at everything as new. You've got a clean slate. That's a beginning."

"You know, there are times when I really hate your optimism."

She laughed. "Me, too. But I'm stuck with it. And as long as you're stuck with me…"

His lips curved into a suggestive smile. "And how long would that be?" he asked.

"Let's start with a month and see how that works."

"A month? With benefits?"

"Everything's negotiable."

Finally, his full-out smile returned. "Is it? Then tell me what you want to take to the bargaining table to open negotiations, and I'll make sure I'm there with whatever you want."

"I'll just bet you will be," she said, swooshing past him and heading toward the beach. Smiling a smile Mateo couldn't see.

She was magnificent, riding the waves. So much beauty and poise skimming over the surface of the water. And in the instant when she disappeared into the wave on her belly, and then emerged standing, balancing herself, she looked like Aphrodite, the goddess of love, or one of the Greek goddesses of the sea.

This was the most uninhibited he'd seen her. It was as though when she became one with the wave she ascended to another place—somewhere ethereal, somewhere that freed her from whatever it was that kept her bound otherwise.

"You ready for your big adventure?" she called as she came walking toward him, her tight black swimsuit emphasizing curves he knew he shouldn't be observing and her wild red hair slicked back, exposing the entirety of her perfect face.

Lizzie dropped her surfboard next to where Mateo was sitting and watching, and picked up one of the bodyboards.

"It's fun in its own right," she said, holding out her empty hand to pull him up.

But he didn't want to move. He'd spent the last hour watching perfection, and that seemed infinitely more interesting than him being out there, flopping around on a bodyboard.

"Truthfully? I'm good, sitting here watching you."

Lizzie dropped down on the huge, multi-colored beach towel with him, grabbed a bottle of water from the small cooler they'd brought, then smiled.

"Because you're a coward?" she taunted.

And her smile was so infectious he caught it in an instant and smiled back.

"Because you're having a good time, and I don't want to interrupt that for what may be some pretty pathetic attempts to keep my belly flat on a board."

Her eyes roamed down to his belly, then back to his face. "Your belly will be fine," she said.

But it wasn't his belly he was concerned about. Other parts were reacting. All the man parts, as he would expect. And most especially his heart.

Was it beating too quickly? Was his breathing coming a little too shallow and fast? It felt that way, and he wasn't even thinking of her in terms of anything that could cause that. It was simply a natural reaction. A primal urge, he wanted to tell himself. Even though he knew it was more than that.

"What about the rest of me?" he asked.

"Do as I say and you won't have any problems. First, for a beginner, it's best to choose a calm spot, where the waves aren't so high. Maybe a couple of feet, but no more than that."

Mateo scooted a little closer to Lizzie, not so much that she would notice, but *he* certainly did.

"Then wax the board. It should already be waxed, but I prefer waxing myself since it's essential to getting a good grip."

"The whole board?" he asked, even though his mind was more on applying sunscreen to her entire body.

"No. Just the top and bottom third, and the edges."

"For a good grip?" he asked.

He was wishing this was more than a simple bodyboarding lesson. Not that he would or could take it anywhere. But something about Lizzie caused him to realize how much he'd missed these past years, and how much he'd forgotten. Smooth skin against his. The touch of delicate fingers. Soft kisses turning wild.

He was putting last night on mental replay and wondering how he was going to manage for the next month. Thinking like this wasn't doing him any good, but he was sure enjoying it. Especially since the object of his attraction—and maybe more—was Lizzie.

He'd never cared much for red hair before; he did remember that. But *her* red hair ignited him. And getting involved with another doctor... That had definitely been off his list, since he knew the ins and outs of that intimately. But he was no longer a doctor, and even if he were it wouldn't matter. Not with Lizzie sitting beside him and their thighs brushing together.

"For staying afloat. Oh, you didn't get yourself a rash guard. Some people like them, because they reduce chafing from the board itself, but maybe that won't bother you."

It wouldn't. Especially if she treated any rash he might get.

"Personally, I like the contact with the board. It gives me a better feel for what I'm doing."

"And the swim fins? The girl at the beach shop said I had to have them."

"Definitely, yes. They'll help you paddle out farther, so you can catch better waves. Oh, and the leash...it attaches to your wrist."

"Seems like an awful lot of trouble just to catch a wave."

"It is—but there's no sensation like it in the world, no matter if you're vertical or horizontal. So, did she sell you a helmet? Black with red stripes?"

"She did."

"And...?"

"And I'll wear it, Lizzie. OK? I'll wear the damned helmet."

He might have argued more with her, but she was so into the moment and he didn't want to break that. She looked beautiful—her eyes sparkling, a slight blush to her cheeks. This was Lizzie in her element, and he was enjoying being there with her even if he didn't so much as get the bottoms of his feet wet.

"Excellent. So, gear up and let's do it. Wade out until you're knee-deep, then put your belly to the board and keep your hips in contact with the tail of the board."

"And my hands?"

He knew where he wanted to put them, but what *he* wanted and what *she* wanted were two different things. Still, he could almost feel her hands skimming down the side of his body, like they had done the night before...

"Top corners of the board. Make sure you

keep your fins under water, then paddle out—one-handed or two, doesn't make a difference—until you see the wave you want to catch. For starters, we're going to catch some smaller ones."

This was getting serious. He needed to get his mind back on what he was about to do, otherwise his amateur performance would turn into a clown show because he'd missed one or two vital steps. Of course, mouth-to-mouth from Lizzie sounded pretty good, if that was what it came down to. Especially now that he knew the secrets of her mouth...

"When you do see a wave, point your board toward the beach and start to kick and paddle. The wave will do the rest."

"Sounds simple enough," he said, looking down the beach at all kinds of people surfing and bodyboarding.

He'd been an adventurer. He remembered that. Remembered scaling rock walls, paragliding, even some dangerous sledding in there. Straight downhill, hoping to avoid the trees and the other sledders. But this? It scared him. Not because of the risk, but because he was, like she'd told him, vulnerable. He didn't know if his adventurous side would come back or if he'd turn into one of those people he could see from where he was, who paddled out and simply sat there on the board, too afraid to move.

"You don't have to do this," Lizzie said.

"I do," he replied, taking off his blue floral print shirt. "In more ways than you know."

To prove it to himself and—more—to prove it to her. That was important…showing Lizzie that side of him—the side that wasn't a patient, that wasn't vulnerable, that wasn't so damned disagreeable. It mattered more than he'd thought it could.

Finally, after another mental bout with himself, he slipped the fins on his feet, grabbed his board, and walked to the water's edge. Lizzie was right there next to him, and he found some strength in having her there. But he hadn't always been this way. That much he remembered.

"It's a simple thing," he said. "I've done much more dangerous things than this. Yet I'm not sure I'm ready to take the next step."

"It's not easy, facing your fears," she said, giving his arm a reassuring squeeze, followed by a tender kiss to his cheek. "Especially when you might not even know what they are until they pop up out of nowhere."

"What scares you?" he asked, looking out over the wide expanse of water.

"Lots of things. Making a medical mistake with one of my patients. That may be my biggest fear, because people rely on me, and if I do something to let them down, or even worse…" She shut her eyes briefly, then shook her head. "Horseback riding. Got thrown when I was a little girl and broke some bones in my back. It wasn't a huge trauma, but to this day I've never been back on a horse. Oh, and spiders. You haven't heard a good scream until you've heard me scream when I find a spider on me— or even near me. And some of the spiders here on Oahu are enormous. Like the cane spider."

She gestured, indicating something larger than a dinner plate, which was an obvious exaggeration, and just saying the word caused her to shiver.

It was a cute display, and something he hadn't expected from her. His version of Lizzie taking on the world had just knocked itself down a peg and he liked seeing that side of her. It made him realize that she had her own vulnerabilities, and that he wouldn't be standing out there alone on that sandbar he could see in the distance, holding on to his own bag of insecurities.

Mateo chuckled. "Well, I'll protect you from spiders if you protect me from myself."

"Do you *need* to be protected from yourself?" she asked.

He took a step into the water, then paused. "If I knew the answer to that I'd tell you."

Then he gathered up every bit of courage inside him and marched out until he was submerged to mid-chest. Lizzie followed him and immediately mounted her board, then waited for Mateo to do the same.

"This isn't too bad," he said, once he was belly-down on the board.

"Paddle around for a few minutes. Get used to the feel of it. Sometimes it's nice to just float for a while and let your mind wander."

"Do you do that?"

"Not so much now," she said, paddling over until her board was next to his. "I did when my dad was alive. He was…difficult. Sometimes it felt like I was failing him even though the doctor in me knew what was happening to him."

She paused for a moment, then continued.

"For me, the ocean has curative powers. When I was a little girl, traveling around with my dad, there were several times we lived near a beach. I think that's where I found my balance."

"So Hawaii was a logical place to come?"

"Actually, I lived here before, when I was a teenager. Dad was getting older, and thinking about retirement in a few years, so he transferred to one of the military hospitals here. It was the first time I ever had much of him in my life—which is one of the reasons I came back when he was diagnosed. Some of my best memories were here, and I remembered how much he'd loved it here as well."

"I'm from a little village in Mexico. The people there were poor. My mother was poor, too, and there wasn't enough work for her. Yet she got a sponsor in California, from one of the humanitarian groups, so we came to the States legally and she achieved her dream—which was to see me succeed."

"And now?" Lizzie asked.

"When I'm ready to travel I'm going back. My mother has the right to know what's happened, since she was a large part of my motivation. It's not going to be easy to tell her, though."

Lizzie laid her hand on his arm and squeezed. "So often the right things aren't. But she'll be glad to know that you're safe, and basically in good shape."

"Maybe you'd like to come with me?"

"I might… Mexico is one place I've never been."

The almost-promise made his heart skip a beat. But taking Lizzie home to meet his mother would be no small deal. The people in the village would throw parties, and sing and dance halfway through the night. There would be piles of food, amazing drinks—and all because Margarita's boy was bringing a woman home. Lizzie would love it, he thought.

"If you go with me, prepare yourself for the biggest party you've ever been to—all in your honor."

"*My* honor?"

"They're a friendly bunch of people. What can I say?"

He wasn't about to tell her that taking her to meet his mother would be as good as a wedding announcement. They weren't ready for that yet. There were still issues to be resolved.

"So, you want to go catch a wave with me now?"

He took in a deep breath. "The waves really are calming, aren't they?"

"And they're calling my name. Mind if I...?"

"Do your thing, Lizzie. I'll be right behind you." Enjoying a view he was pretty sure he wanted to enjoy for the rest of his life.

In preparation to catch a good wave she paddled out a little farther, and found the perfect one that carried her almost all the way back to the shore. It seemed so natural for her. And for him? Well...he paddled out, like she did, found his wave, aimed his board, and rode the wave as best he could, weaving and bobbing in and out of the water until he almost hit shore.

"Wasn't as graceful as you," he said, spitting out a mouthful of saltwater as he stood and grabbed his board. "But that was fun. Thank you."

Lizzie smiled at him. "All part of the service offered to my houseguests. Want to go again?"

"How about I sit here and watch *you* go again?"

"Whatever you want," she said, turning and walking back into the water.

Mateo shut his eyes as the headache overtook him again. It had come and gone for days now, but this one was excruciating, pounding harder and harder, until suddenly everything around him was spinning. The sky, the sand, the water. Himself.

He turned to look for Lizzie, who was just emerging from the water, and waved her over.

"Migraine," he said as she approached.

The brightness of the sun was bothering him. And a wave of nausea pounded him so hard he fell backwards into the sand.

"Not good, Lizzie," he managed to gasp as she dropped to her knees next to him. "Not good at all."

"Has this happened before?" she asked as she felt for his pulse.

"Yes, but not as bad."

"And you didn't bother mentioning it?"

"It's a headache. Everybody gets them."

* * *

She pulled back his eyelids and studied his eyes for a moment, wishing she had her medical bag. His pupillary response was sluggish, and the size from right to left varied, but not by much. It was clear something was wrong, but she couldn't risk leaving him here like this to go get her medical bag.

He grasped her hand. "I think I might be in trouble here," he said, holding on tight.

"I need to get you to the hospital so we can get a scan to see what's going on."

"For a freaking migraine?" he snapped, then clearly instantly regretted his tone of voice. "Just let me stay here and I'll be better in a few minutes."

"Unless it's not a simple migraine. I mean, I don't think it's a stroke, nor is some kind of neuro inflammation at the top of my list, but it could be another clot. Most definitely you've got some changes in brain activity that underlie the chronic pain you've been having, and my best guess—which is all I have at the moment—is that it's connected to your earlier brain trauma. So I can leave you here in the sand and hope it doesn't advance to another level, like a stroke, or I can get you to the hospital to see what's really going on. Your choice, Mateo."

"You know…that's the thing I most dislike about doctors. They take it to the limit."

"How do you mean?"

"It's a migraine. I've diagnosed them and treated them. But you're thinking way beyond that, aren't you?"

"That's why they pay me the big bucks. I'm very good at thinking way beyond what's normal or necessary."

He laughed, then moaned and grabbed his head. "Look, Lizzie. I appreciate the concern, but it's a stinking headache. That's all."

"I hope you're right about that, but in case you're not are you sure you want me to walk away and leave you with an unconfirmed diagnosis?"

She moved closer to him, took his hand, and bent down to kiss him on the lips.

Just before the kiss, she whispered, "I really don't want to lose you, Mateo, and it's not because I'm a doctor who hates losing patients. It's because I'm a woman who doesn't want to lose the man she's falling in love with."

She still needed to figure out how that would play out, as none of her feelings of trepidation had changed. But that was a discussion for another day. Right now, all she wanted was to get Mateo better.

"And if you make the wrong decision and I walk away…it would break my heart. I don't want that happening and I don't deserve it."

That much was true.

That she loved him was also true.

"Get me to the hospital and give me the scan," he said, trying to open his eyes, but failing, as if the sun nauseated him. "Do whatever you think needs to be done."

Blowing out a sigh of relief, Lizzie made the call, then sat there holding his hand while they waited.

One thing was sure. A life with Mateo wouldn't always be smooth. But it would always be good. And she hoped they could get to that point. Because after Mateo there wouldn't be anybody else. For all his stubborn ways, he was the only one she wanted.

When the time was right, she'd tell him. But there were issues to work out before any kind of commitment could be made, and those issues scared her. Neither of them came to this relationship unscathed. Two wounded people... Could that work?

"Are you going to hold my hand when they send me through that long tube of extreme claustrophobia?" he asked.

They were in the changing room and he was expected to put on one of those hideous gowns.

"Seriously? You're claustrophobic?"

"Maybe a little."

She tied him modestly into the green and blue gown he hated so much, then gave him a blanket to spread over his lap as they wheeled him down the hall—*in a wheelchair*—for his tests.

"I always tell my patients the best thing for that is a shot of vodka—*after* the procedure."

"Hate the stuff," he said, reaching out to take Lizzie's hand once they were in the waiting room.

"Sex works, too," she whispered. "Depending on the diagnosis."

"*Now* we're getting somewhere."

Lizzie was worried and trying to hide it. He

could see her struggle. She wasn't very good at hiding her expressions from him.

"It's going to be a migraine, pure and simple. You do know that, don't you?"

"No, I don't." Lizzie sat next to Mateo, holding his hand as the technicians prepared him for a CT scan. "Look, this isn't going to take long, then if nothing shows we can go home and you can spend the rest of the day sleeping. Now, I'm going to run down to Janis's office for a minute and have a quick chat with her, if you don't mind?"

"Go," he whispered, as if the sound of his own voice hurt him.

"Two minutes—tops," she said, bending over the hard, flat CT table to give him a kiss. "I'll be right back."

She hated leaving him there, but there was nothing else she could do. She needed distance, and a couple of minutes to sort out her feelings. And some reassurance.

"You've got it bad, don't you?" said Janis, joining Lizzie, who was leaning on the wall outside the CT room.

"Depends on your definition of 'bad,'" Lizzie

said. "Do I have feelings for him? Yes. What kind of feelings? Not the kind I should be having. Oh, and he didn't want to have this CT," she said.

"Did it occur to you that the man is so scared he doesn't know what he's doing? I mean, to look at him you'd never guess that, but Mateo is…*different*. He's a healer who can no longer heal. He has no home, no place to go, no plans for his future. If I were in his shoes, I'd be scared, too."

"I think he wanted to die."

"He wants to live, Lizzie. He just doesn't know how. If he had a death wish he wouldn't have showed up on your doorstep. To Mateo, you offer hope. And loving him the way I'm pretty sure you do is an added bonus he didn't count on. So give the guy some slack. Back off when he needs it, and stay close when that's what he wants."

Janis's words rang in her head as she made her way back to Mateo. It wasn't just Mateo who was resistant, though. Or scared.

"So, you ready to get this done?" she asked, as the tech wheeled him into the room and helped him take his position on the CT bed. "Ten minutes and it'll all be over."

"Or starting again," he said.

Lizzie swallowed hard. "If that's how it turns out we'll work through it. I'm not going anywhere, Mateo. So if you start over this time you start with someone in your corner."

She bent down to kiss him, but he caught her off-guard and pulled her almost on top of him, gave her the kiss of a lifetime.

"That was…nice," she said, pulling back from him. "But maybe not appropriate here."

He grinned up at her. "That's just me being true to character."

"Has anyone ever told you you're incorrigible?"

"Has anyone ever *not* told me I'm incorrigible?"

"Dr. Peterson?" blared a voice from the microphone in the next room. "We need to get on with this test. Dr. Sanchez isn't our only patient."

"But way to go," Janis added through the same microphone.

"Now look what you've done," Lizzie said to Mateo as she left the room, fanning herself.

Rather than join her colleagues in the control room, she went to her office to wait, dropped down on the sofa, and shut her eyes until Janis came to talk to her.

"It's a small hemorrhage. Same place as before."

"Because we went bodyboarding?" Lizzie asked, as tears tickled the backs of her eyes.

"I'd say the first injury simply caused a weak spot. I think this would have happened no matter what he was doing."

"I wasn't cautious enough—just like I wasn't cautious enough with my dad." Finally the tears overflowed, and she batted at them with the back of her hand. "Have you admitted him?"

"We're in the process. Then we're going to fix him—hopefully for good this time."

"With a drip?"

"Clot-busters save lives. And I think there's a lot of life in Mateo that needs saving. And guiding."

"Not my responsibility," Lizzie said.

"When you love somebody the way you do Mateo, *everything* about him is your responsibility. It changes your world, Lizzie. Nothing's the same anymore. But because Mateo is a sick man, you're the one who must step up and assume more than responsibility. You need to step up and accept his love—because he does love you."

"We have a long way to go before either of us can do anything. But I suppose now's as good a time as any to get started."

"*After* the procedure, please. This is Mateo I've got to deal with, and you know how he can be."

She did—and that was a large part of why she loved him. To her, Mateo was nearly perfect. Sure, there were some flaws. But they were such a small part of him, while his kindness and compassion embraced most of him.

Maybe Janis didn't see that, but *she* did, and that was all that really mattered.

Janis took off her surgical mask and threw it in the trash on her way out to see Lizzie. "It's done. He's sleeping peacefully. I need a tropical drink. Care to join me on my lanai?"

"Could I have a raincheck?" Lizzie asked. "I think I'd like to go sit in his room for a while."

"He's mumbling nonsense," Janis warned her. "Something about letting it happen. I'm assuming that means you?"

"I hope it does," she said, then headed off to Mateo.

"Janis says everything went well," she said, sitting down next to his bed. "You've got a catheter in your head, which will stay there several days, but the clot was small and likely just a residual from your initial injury."

He opened his eyes to look at her, managed a lazy smile, then went back to sleep. But he held on to her hand for dear life, and she vowed to stay right there with him until the anesthesia wore off and they were bringing him that green slime they commonly referred to as gelatin.

She recalled his first day there, when he'd asked her to please put on the first page of his chart that he loathed and detested green gelatin—or any gelatin, for that matter. And cottage cheese.

She'd never quite gotten around to doing that.

Lizzie laughed, even though nothing in her felt like laughing.

"Toward the end, Mateo," she said, even though he wasn't awake, "my dad only ate things with bright colors. I suppose he thought the color had something to do with the taste. But when they brought him his tray, if it didn't have something red or yellow or purple on it he wouldn't eat it."

She looked up, watched his heart monitor for a minute, and noticed how perfect his rhythm was. He was a strong man. This would only be a minor setback for him.

"Oh, you're back in your old room. Thought you'd appreciate being here…for old times' sake." She gave his hand a squeeze. "And your old hospital gowns are ready for you, too."

"Do you ever stop talking?" he asked, even though he didn't open his eyes.

"Does it bother you?" she asked, glad to hear his voice sounding so clear.

"No. It lets me know I'm alive and have something to look forward to."

"What?" she asked breathlessly, thinking of all the things he might say. Hoping *she* topped his list.

"Green gelatin."

* * *

"Funny thing is, I didn't even know it was happening. It kind of crept up on me, a little at a time."

She was sitting on the lanai with Janis, sipping something fruity from an original brown tiki cup. Janis was sipping something fruity from her favorite pink pineapple. It was late into evening now, and Mateo was still sleeping like a baby while she was trying to figure out the next step.

"I gave his case back to Randy," Janis informed her. "He's not as tolerant as you, so if you know what's good for your boyfriend you'll warn him to shape up or he'll be kicked out of here one more time."

*Her boyfriend.* Lizzie liked the sound of that.

What would come of it? She didn't know.

But right now that didn't matter.

She had a brick wall to scale before she could do anything.

His head hurt like a son of a gun, and to make matters worse there were five containers of green slime on his bedside table. Just looking at them jiggling at him made him feel nauseated. So did the hospital gown and the no-slide booties someone had slipped on his feet.

"This isn't the way life is meant to be lived," he said to Lizzie as she entered his room.

"They told me you were awake and in your usual good humor." She gave him a quick kiss, then sat down on the edge of the bed. "Has Janis been in to see you yet?"

"Nobody's been in to see me except the green gelatin fairy and you."

"Well, the news is good. The clot was small. It probably resulted from a weak suture put in on the first surgery. And your recovery can be done at my house, if that's what you want."

"What I want is for you to listen to me, and then tell me if I'm right or wrong."

"About what?"

"Your feelings for me. You're in love with me—or I hope you're in love with me—but it scares you because of what happened to your father. You're not sure you can get involved with someone with memory loss again."

"That's very perceptive," she said.

"But is it true, Lizzie?"

"Some of it is. You aren't the same as he

was, but sometimes when I see that lost look in your eyes…"

"Have you seen it lately?"

She paused for a minute to think about it. "Not really."

"Your dad's illness wasn't your fault, Lizzie."

He reached for her hand, then pulled her closer to him until they were almost lying side by side.

"I know that. But…"

She bit down on her lip, willing herself not to cry.

"It was a really hectic day. He wanted to go for a walk and I didn't have time. I didn't let his caregivers do it because it was about the only way Dad and I were connecting, and I didn't want to be cheated of that. I promised him we'd go later…like he understood what I was saying. About an hour later I got the call to say that Dad had wandered off. It wasn't the first time, but he always headed toward the ocean, and I was so afraid… Well, we searched the shore for hours and there was no sign of him. The search continued for five days. *Five days*, Mateo. He was out there lost and alone for five days. And then the rescuers found him.

He'd gone to Kapu Falls, which was one of his favorite places. He'd actually planted a flower garden there."

"Nobody went there to look?"

"Actually, they did. But Dad had crawled into some underbrush and apparently gone to sleep. At least that was what the coroner said. And he stayed in that same spot for five days. Maybe because that's where he wanted to die, or maybe he was simply waiting for me to come take him home. We'll never know."

She clenched her fists and shut her eyes.

"That's the nightmare I live with every day. And there are so many what-ifs. What if I hadn't gone to work? What if we'd taken the walk he wanted to take? What if the caregiver hadn't turned her back? What if I had one more lock put on all the doors?"

"It's impossible to predict outcomes all the time, Lizzie. Sometimes you're right, but as often as not you're wrong."

"Exactly, Mateo. You can't always predict outcomes."

"Meaning?"

"Meaning that at some point you've got to get on with your life or it will bury you. I was being buried. Not sure what I wanted to do. Yet the answer was always there. I was the one who had to open my eyes and see it, though."

"And the answer?"

"You, me…a beachside clinic. You can't operate anymore, and that may be a reality for the rest of your life. I think you've probably figured out that I've lost the heart for working in a hospital. I want a simpler life, and life's too short not to go after what you want."

"You said you and me in that clinic?"

"The reality is, for now, you'll have to be supervised. I can't predict the future, and I'm not even sure I would if I could. But you're a good doctor and you deserve to be back in medicine. Maybe it's not the way you want, but it's what you can have. And perhaps that's all we really need…what we can have. I think we could build a life around that, if you want to."

"Me as patient, you as caregiver?"

"No. That's not at all what I want."

"Then, as your equal. Someone you don't have to watch day and night. Or at work."

"Why are you twisting this, Mateo? I thought…" She shook her head. "Have I been wrong about this all long?"

"You took in a homeless guy, Lizzie. What's there to twist in that?"

"I thought I took in someone who wanted more from life. Was I wrong?"

She was battling gallantly against the tears that wanted to fall. To finally admit her feelings, then have them slapped back in her face… she couldn't even begin to describe the pain.

"No, you weren't wrong. But I've given it a lot of thought, and…" He paused, drew in a deep breath, then let it out again, agonizingly slow. "And I don't see how it could work with us. I don't want to be taken care of, like you took care of your dad, and I'm sure that's not what you want either. But I'm afraid it's inevitable. Also, I don't want to be watched for the rest of my life, with you wondering if it's the real me when I make a little slip-up. It's got nothing to do with the way I feel for you and everything to do with breathing room."

"I haven't been giving you *breathing room*?"

"You have. As much as I can handle right now. But in the future…"

"You don't have to say it, Mateo. What I saw as the beginning of something that might last was merely a port in the storm for you. But

I'm glad I put myself out there for you—because it proved to me that I can do it. It was my choice, and it had nothing to do with my dad." She got up from the bed. "I'll have your things brought to the hospital, Mateo."

"This isn't what I want, Lizzie. I want to figure out how we can be together—not apart."

"What you want, Mateo, is a life that doesn't come with the complications we both have. That's what I wanted at first as well. But we don't always get what we want, do we? Oh, and as for falling in love—it shouldn't be about figuring out how to do it. It should be about how you can't live without the other person. How loving the other person makes you a better person. I'm sorry it didn't work that way for you, because it did for me."

He started to get out of bed, but he was connected to too many wires and tubes, and the instant he tried to stand every single one of the alarms went off.

"I do love you," he said as she headed for the door. "It's just that—"

"And that's where it ends, Mateo. After you tell someone you love them there should be no more words. No qualifiers. But you have a qualifier, and that says it all. I'm sorry this didn't work, because I love you, too."

With that, she was gone.

And he was stuck in a lousy hospital bed, with a tray full of green gelatin which he wanted to throw at the wall.

But he didn't. That was the Mateo who had existed *before* Lizzie. The one who existed after her merely shoved the bedside tray away, slunk down in bed, and pulled the sheets up to his neck.

# CHAPTER NINE

*Eight weeks later*

MORNINGS WERE NOT her friend. Especially now, when she spent every one of them being sick and looking puffy. It was part of the process, her doctor had told her, but that meant nothing when she was sprawled on the bathroom floor, glad for the cool feel of the tile underneath her.

"Come on, Lizzie!" Janis yelled through the door. "It's perfectly natural. If you spend your entire pregnancy this way, by the time the baby gets here you're going to be a basket case."

"Babies!" she yelled back. "Not baby. When he got me, he got me good."

Janis opened the door a crack and peeked in. "You're not even dressed."

"Not getting dressed today."

"So what do I tell your patients?"

"That pregnancy and doctoring don't mix."

Janis pushed the door the rest of the way open and went in. She sat down next to Lizzie, who still wasn't budging.

"Someone should have told me," she moaned.

"Ever hear about using protection?"

"We did. It didn't work—*obviously*." Lizzie rolled over on her back but still didn't get up. "See how big I am and I'm only two months in. Do you really think I'm in any shape to see patients? I mean, I'm wearing a *muumuu*, Janis. A freaking muumuu."

"Get used to it. The bigger you get, the more you'll come to appreciate your muumuu. Oh, and if you want another, I hear there's a mighty handsome man working in a surf shop a couple blocks over from the hospital. In case you didn't know, he stayed here, Lizzie. He's working hard with a PTSD counselor, as well as sticking to Randy's cognitive behavior program. I'll bet he'd like to see you."

"He knows where I live." Lizzie wrestled herself to a sitting position and leaned against the wall.

"Doesn't he have a right to know about the babies?" Janis asked.

"He does—and he will. But he's so deep

into his treatment programs now I wonder if I should wait, rather than throw him another curve ball he has to deal with."

"Have your feelings for him changed?" Janis asked her.

Lizzie patted her belly. "No. In fact, they're growing deeper every day."

"And you expect to work things out sprawled here on the floor in a muumuu?"

"There's a lot to work out," Lizzie said, finally ready to get up.

"Do you know who you sound like?" Janis asked, pushing herself up and heading toward the door.

"No. Who?"

"Mateo. Do you remember when he was full of excuses, not doing anything to help himself, and everybody was getting frustrated with him?"

Lizzie thought about it as she pushed herself off the floor. "I didn't accept his excuses, did I?"

Janis gave her a knowing wink, then left.

And Lizzie put on some regular clothes and decided a walk was in order.

Funny how that walk took her right by a surf

shop, where the clerk inside was keeping a whole line of people entertained with stories of his days as a surfer. Like he'd ever even *been* on a real surfboard.

It was such a funny sight, Lizzie laughed… probably for the first time in weeks. This was the father of her babies—the man she loved despite his faulty memories.

Lizzie waved at Mateo when he finally spotted her in the crowd, then waited until he made his way through the crowd to smile at him.

"Looks like you've found your calling," she said, fighting back a laugh. "Talking about your exploits from your days as a surfer?"

"Give the people what they want," he said, taking her by the arm and leading her out of the crowd. "I've wanted to see you. To talk to you about that day. I was overwhelmed, Lizzie. I hope you realize that?"

"You could have come around to apologize," she said, as they sat down on a bench under a banyan tree.

"I did. Every day. Who do you think has been tending your dad's flower garden?"

"I never saw you. And as for the garden…

I just…" She shrugged. "I didn't give it any thought."

"Which is why it was getting weedy, and droopy from a lack of watering. I know I hurt you, Lizzie. And I'm sorry for that. But for a while I couldn't live with myself, let alone draw somebody else into my mess. I needed time…and space."

"And?"

"And I've been doing everything I can so that when I finally came back to you, hat in hand if that's how I had to do it, you'd see the differences in me. I wasn't good enough for you then. Maybe not even now. But I'm working on it. Trying new things where old things I've forgotten used to be."

"Like working in a surf shop?"

"If that's what it takes. I know there's a lot I won't get back, and I'm trying hard to come to terms with that. Some days are better than others. Occasionally I get so damned frustrated that all I want to do is go someplace and turn myself into somebody else. Like my surfer persona."

"But you stayed?"

"Because I have to. Because I fell in love

with the most wonderful, stubborn, and opin-
ionated woman I've ever known, and to walk
away from that would be the worst thing I
could ever do in my life. I'm trying hard to fix
myself for *me*, Lizzie. But it's also for you. For
a future where you won't have to worry about
me every minute of every day. For the time
when I leave the house and you won't have to
pace the lanai and wonder what's happening
to me. You deserve that, Lizzie. We both do.
But I'm the one who has to fix that. And I'm
trying." He brushed her cheek with the back
of his hand. "I stayed because I want to prove
myself to you. Prove that I'm everything you
need and want."

"You have been, Mateo. Every day since I
met you. I mean, it hasn't been easy, and I've
some adjusting to do myself, but living all
these weeks without you…it's been miserable.
I've been miserable. And that's not how I want
to be. Especially now, because I need an *equal*,
Mateo. I mean, we can't predict the future, but
we can live for what we have today, and that's
what I need. I thought so at first, anyway. But
then my need changed into something I wanted
more than anything I'd ever wanted in my life,

and I didn't see you getting involved in that. In fact, you pushed me away."

"Because I'm not sure yet who I am, and I still get frustrated when I can't pull up a memory. I'm working hard at dealing with myself, but that still adds up to a lifetime of misery for you, and I don't want that."

"Not misery, Mateo. Not if you love someone enough. The way I love you. What I finally realized was that your belligerence is only your way of trying to hang on to the pieces of you that you remember. You're fighting back."

"And I'm scared, Lizzie. Scared to death. But having you there made things better. And my memory of that night in Afghanistan…" He pointed to his head, "I do remember it now. Every bloody detail. How my friends tried to rescue me and died. How I lost my best friend. How I laid there for two days before anybody found me. It's not a pretty thing to recall, but it's my memory, which means it's part of me. And I've found other parts as well. Some good, some not so good. For better or worse, all of it me, though. And as these bits and pieces are returning, they give me something to hold on to. You give me more, though, and I want to earn my way back into your life. Unless I blew it too badly to fix."

"You didn't blow anything, Mateo. I think we were always just two people fighting to get through to each other. Sometimes succeeding, sometimes not." She took hold of his hand and laid it on her belly. "And sometimes going farther than any expectation either of us had."

"Seriously?" he asked. "You're…?"

"Eight weeks along. Healthy and grumpy. Having some battles with my hormones."

"Do you know if it's a boy or a girl?"

"Could be one of each…"

"I did all that?" he said, his pride obvious.

"It took two of us, Mateo. I did have a part in this."

He laughed out loud. "And here I was thinking that being alone, while it isn't good, isn't as bad as I thought it was. I'm assuming you want me involved?"

"I'm wearing muumuus, Mateo. And eating everything in the house. Does that sound like a person who doesn't want her baby daddy involved? Someone has to save me from myself—especially since for breakfast this morning I ate a whole mango pie."

"The whole thing?"

She nodded. "Would have eaten another one if I'd had it."

"Sounds to me like you're going to need that muumuu."

"Not as much as I need you. Will you come home, Mateo? The babies and I need you there. And, more than that, I want you there."

In answer, he pulled her into his arms and kissed her, while across the street Janis sat at an outside café with Randy, watching the whole thing.

"Looks to me like we're about to lose one of our doctors," she said. "I think our Lizzie is about to become otherwise occupied."

# EPILOGUE

As WEDDINGS WENT, Lizzie and Mateo's was a small, private affair. Janis stood up for Lizzie and Randy stood for Mateo. They were in the flower garden, surrounded by all the beautiful flowers her dad had planted. Definitely paradise in so many ways.

For the ceremony Lizzie held Robert, named for her dad, while Mateo held Margarita, named for his mother. The twins were six months old now, just getting to the age where they had their own opinions—which were sometimes a bit vocal.

"I think Robert needs changing," Lizzie said.

"And Margarita seems like she's hungry," her soon-to-be husband responded. "Maybe we should take care of that before the ceremony begins, so we're not interrupted partway through."

"Especially since we've waited so long for this."

She looked back at the small crowd gathering, and at Janis passing out tiki cups full of whatever her concoction of the day was. No one was left without a tiki.

"I think Janis has everything under control for a few minutes."

Lizzie and Mateo dashed into the house to take care of the twins, who'd become the center of so many lives since, for now, they went to work every day with Mateo. Not to the surf shop, but to the clinic they'd bought. He and Lizzie worked there full-time, loving the life, loving the work.

The clinic was busier than ever, with more and more patients coming through the door every day. The addition of a nursery was a blessing, as Mateo refused to be separated from his family, and now Dr. Lizzie Peterson-soon-to-be-Sanchez was a part of that.

Lizzie still had a way to go in not taking on the blame for her dad's death, but Mateo was always there to help her through the rough spots. And she was always there when his memory lapses gave way to frustration.

"He's going to be here today, you know," Mateo said. "Since we're marrying in his garden."

"Sometimes it's like I feel him here, looking after his flowers. He would be happy knowing you're the one doing that now."

She brushed a tear from her eyes and looked over at Mateo, who had a spit-up towel slung over his shoulder and was holding a baby who was happily indulging in a bottle.

"Guess I should feed Robert, too," she said, tossing another spit-up towel over her own shoulder and giving him his own bottle.

And that was how they walked down the path to the trellis where they would take their wedding vows. A family of four. Everything Lizzie had never known she wanted. Everything she would ever need.

One husband, two children, and paradise.

The perfect life.

\* \* \* \* \*

# LET'S TALK

## *Romance*

For exclusive extracts, competitions and special offers, find us online:

f facebook.com/millsandboon

⊚ @millsandboonuk

🐦 @millsandboon

Or get in touch on 0844 844 1351*

For all the latest titles coming soon, visit millsandboon.co.uk/nextmonth